No part of this publication may be reproduced, stored in a retrieval system, or transmitted in any form or by any means, electronic, mechanical, photocopying, recording, scanning, or otherwise, without the prior written permission of the publisher, except in the case of brief quotations within critical reviews and otherwise as permitted by copyright law.

NOTE: This is a work of fiction. Names, characters, places, and incidents are a product of the author's imagination. Any resemblance to real life is purely coincidental. All characters in this story are 18 or older.

Copyright © 2020, Willow Winters Publishing. All rights reserved.

Delilah

Second of a Trilogy

USA TODAY BESTSELLING AUTHOR

To my husband.

My hero and my love.

"It's so much darker when a light goes out than it would have been if it had never shone."

- John Steinbeck

USA Today Best Selling Author, Willow Winters, brings you an all-consuming, sizzling romance featuring an epic, anti-hero you won't soon forget.

Some love stories are a slow burn. Others are quick to ignite, scorching and branding your very soul before you've taken that first breath. You're never given a chance to run from it. That's how I'd describe what happened to us.

Everything around me blurred and all that existed were his lips, his touch…
The chase and the heat between us became addictive.
Our nights together were a distraction, one we craved to the point of letting the world crumble around us.
We should have paid more attention; we should have known that it would come to this.
We both knew it couldn't last, but that didn't change what we desired most.

All we wanted was each other…

Prologue

Marcus
Twenty-One Years Ago

It's warmer in the barn. Here in the corner, nestled in the hay, it's far warmer than it is outside. More importantly, in this back corner, there's not a place for the brutal wind to slip in. The tips of my fingers could just as well be pieces of ice tucked under my chin as I hunker down in the hay. It smells like dirt and pigs, but the warmth is more comforting than anything I've felt in days. By the looks of it, there hasn't been a soul here in quite some time.

I spent the past three nights outside. Last night I dug into the ground to try to hide from the vicious wind that whipped through my tattered clothes. The hard earth was like a brick of clay and it took far too much energy to dig deep enough. It helped, but my throat is sore, my body is weak and

I don't know that I'll ever get my hands warm again. There's only one thing I'm certain of: I can't keep going on like this. Something has to give.

Late fall in the northeast turns frigid sooner than most cities. My teacher used to refer to all the backwoods towns off the highway outside of New York City as Podunk. So that's what I've been calling them all, the Podunk towns. I don't even know where I am other than somewhere deep in the woods but to the left of the farms. It's open fields out there, wide open with nowhere to hide.

This barn looks abandoned, a lonely decrepit place, and perfect for one night. Just one night to close my eyes and get the strength to keep moving. I don't know how far I'll run, but he told me his home was past the Podunk towns and that's where mine used to be ... if only I can find it.

When I close my eyes and ignore the smells, all I can hear is his voice. I try to forget the worst parts and only think about the stories he told me. He had so many good ones about his mother and how she was going to find us and save us. I remember how sure he was whenever he said we were safe. It was the only way I could sleep although I would have never admitted that to him. I was the one who was supposed to be protecting him, not the other way around. Safety surrounds me for a moment; a long enough moment that my eyes feel heavy and my body sags against the barn wood, begging me to give in to much-needed sleep.

Every muscle still burns from running. Even worse so because I ran up the mountain and into the thick, dense forest when I heard the cars coming. I won't let them get me too. I'll never be caught again. Each little cut stings and seems to sear the memories into my skin with every small movement, but I focus on the stories ... the good ones he told. The ones that almost made us smile, the ones that made us forget where we were.

Sleep nearly takes me ... almost there.

Until a sudden creak forces my tired eyes wide open and my heart races, listening to a man pry open the doors of the barn.

Chapter 1

Delilah

My father always told me to trust my gut. He also said when someone shows you who they are, believe them. It's always made sense to me, as has most of my father's wisdom, and from the day he gave me that piece of advice until now, I've lived by that motto.

Right now, though, as I stare into Cody's eyes, listening to him reassure me that I know everything he does about the cold cases and about Marcus, I doubt myself. I thought I knew him. I thought wrong. The man I know Cody Walsh to be is nowhere around and a stranger stares back at me.

I find myself in his home feeling anything but secure. He's lying to me. It's the only thing I'm certain of and I can't even begin to process how much it hurts. Of everyone I've worked with to solve these cases, I trusted him the most. I've leaned on him for years and right now, I question everything.

Men have secrets, my mother used to whisper. Back then I thought she was the crazy one. Now I'm wondering if I inherited that trait as well.

"I'm telling you," Cody says, starting up again, bringing my gaze back to his. "You're worked up and I don't blame you, but there's nothing I know that you don't." His voice is calm and comforting, but his eyes are flat and devoid of commitment. It's like they want me to know he doesn't mean a damn word he's saying.

My tired body begs me to give in to Cody, to just believe him and shake off the horrible gut-wrenching feelings that seep from the marrow of my bones. Every time I close my eyes, though, I see the picture of the boy. The statements. The death certificate.

"I don't think you believe me," Cody says when I don't answer him. The sizzle of the thick slice of ham he places in the frying pan brings me back to the present. It's pitch black outside, but still the streetlights filter in through the curtains in Cody's dining room.

With my arms crossed, I lean my hip against the counter and I have to clear my tight throat before telling him again, "It's just that I feel like there's more to it." Shame washes over me. I should tell him I went through his things. I should confess that much and maybe he'd confess too.

"Because the cases haven't been solved. Every case I've ever had that went cold ... I've felt like that," he says, speaking to the stove instead of me, flipping the ham and then scooping potatoes from the back pan onto the two simple white plates beside the stove.

Even with my sanity stretched far too thin, somewhere in the back of my exhausted mind I'm fully aware that I should be grateful for Cody and that, as far as I know, he doesn't have any reason at all to lie to me. I can't shake this feeling, though. My gut instinct is that he's lying ... it also whispers that I should keep what I know hidden from him just the same. One old case file I opened while I was snooping has shifted everything.

He continues, "Because there *is* more to it. To all of those cases we didn't close. You and I both know that." He adds under his breath, so low I almost don't hear, "There's more to all those cases."

With a deep thump in my chest that ricochets a pain that can't possibly compare to his, a flash of the photo I found comes to mind. The black and white photo of Cody and his brother standing with an older man, maybe their uncle since they resembled him closely. The image is followed with more thoughts of the case that was never fully closed. At least not for him.

The silverware clinks against the porcelain as he places a plate in front of me, not missing a beat of his explanation.

"Of course you feel like there's more. There is more; I just don't know that we'll ever know the truth."

My gaze flies to his, but he isn't looking at me. He's focused on spearing the ham and eating, like I should do. Lord knows I've had more to drink than I needed tonight.

With every swallow, questions beg to be spoken.

I barely taste the meal, although the heavy scent of butter and pork makes me believe it should be delicious.

"We may never know the truth, but we did everything we could." Cody's statement carries a note of finality. As if it's the end of the conversation.

A sadness washes over me. I'm sure that's what he thinks about his brother's case and it tears me up inside to imagine him as a young boy, being handed paperwork and most likely, told little lies to lessen the blow of what happened to his younger brother.

We did everything we could. I've heard it so many times. Everything isn't always good enough though, is it?

"Eat something." Cody's command sounds more like a plea. He even wears a half smile, as if smiling would make the thoughts in my mind disappear.

The atmosphere changes when his gaze softens. "Delilah, baby," he says, dropping his fork and striding toward me to pin me between him and the counter. A hand rests on either side of me, but he doesn't touch me. "You haven't slept, I'm guessing?" he says and he guesses right. "I know you haven't eaten."

The way he cares for me, obviously trying to console me, destroys that nagging bit inside that believes he's being deceitful.

"You need sleep." With a single kiss on my forehead, suddenly my mother's warning fades and I remember what my father told me. I trust my instincts from years ago, when I first met and fell for this man. My gut back then said that I could love him. And the part about secrets? Well, just like I told my mother back then, we all have them.

I share one of them right now. "I'll have nightmares," I say, whispering the confession, feeling a flurry of fear run through me.

Cody's eyes flash with shock and then he rests a hand on my chin. "Is that why you aren't sleeping?" With both of my hands I pull his away, kissing his knuckles and nodding against his chest.

Leaning into him, it's easy to close my eyes.

He's gentle as he holds me, rubbing soothing circles on my back and the fight ... or whatever that was a moment ago seems to vanish. Disappearing like it never happened.

He plants small kisses along the crown of my head and tells me, "You're going through hell. You're stressed and it's killing you."

My eyes slowly open and I stare at the curtains as the panel on the right sways gently from the air exiting the floor vent beneath it.

"I know," I say and it's all I admit. It feels like I'm drowning, but there isn't an ounce of water to baptize my sinful soul in.

There's a rumble in Cody's chest, deep and masculine when I lift up my lips and kiss his throat, right against his Adam's apple. The stubble there tickles the tip of my nose.

A contented sigh leaves him and so I do it again.

I let him feel the hint of my smile against his hot skin when the growing erection he has becomes more than obvious.

"Look at what you do to me," he groans, as if it's an apology or perhaps like I'm torturing him.

"How about you fuck me to sleep," I suggest, wanting nothing more than just that. "Make me forget it all." My murmur pleads with him and in an instant, a yelp is ripped from me as he lifts me by my ass and sets me on the kitchen counter.

The sudden movement has my heart racing but the heat is all from the longing look in his steely blue gaze.

"Now that I can handle," he says before capturing my lips with his. His touch is strong, unrelenting and easy to get lost in. With his right hand steady on my hip, his left roams up my shirt and lingers over the curve of my waist. I wrap my legs around his hips and press my feet against his ass so I can feel his hard length against my core.

I'm shameless as I grind against him. I only break the kiss to take a breath of cool air, but Cody doesn't take the moment to pause. He continues his relentless touches, trailing his warm lips down my neck and kissing along every inch. My nipples pebble as a moan slips from my lips.

"Please," I beg him. And that single word is his undoing.

"Not here," he says as he lifts me into his arms and I cling to his broad frame while he takes me to his bed.

When he's done with me, after fucking me until I scream his name and forcing my release from me, I thought he'd done exactly what I'd asked: to fuck me to sleep and make me forget it all. I thought he had, but he didn't. Sleep eludes me and all I can see are the palest of blue eyes watching me from a memory in the dark night, judging and waiting.

Cody's eyes close faster than mine and even though my lungs beg me to breathe in time with him, the sound of his inhales and exhales so soothing, I can't fall asleep.

I can still feel him inside of me as I slip out of his bed. Leaving the warm sheets behind, I let out a small hum of satisfaction at the hint of pain and pleasure that lingers.

I'm quiet as I slip out, gathering a chair from the dining room and bringing it to the hall closet so I can have just one more look. Sitting cross-legged in the early morning on a hallway floor, plagued by insomnia, digging through a box of a lover's darkest moments ... that's certainly not anything I ever thought I'd be striving toward. Yet here I am, obsessing over doing exactly that.

As I reach up to the box, my shirt lifting, I'm only vaguely aware of the floor creaking behind me. With my mind focused on the little boy in the photo labeled with the names of two brothers with their uncle, and what exactly each of those papers tells me about him and maybe little hints of what made Cody the man he is, it doesn't register.

My subconscious is aware that someone is behind me, but my desire for the truth is greedy and requires answers.

"Those aren't yours." The single sentence is chilling. With my heart slamming into my throat, I whip around to face Cody, nearly falling off the chair. Caught red-handed.

What makes matters worse is that his eyes look how mine feel. Exhausted and spent. The remainder of his expression, though, is hard and lacking forgiveness.

Swallowing thickly, I tell him, "I'm sorry."

"I mean it, Delilah." Cody's pale blue eyes hold a warning as he adds, "Everyone has their boundaries."

Chapter 2

Marcus

The majority of people in Delilah's hometown, a staggering ninety-two percent, are born in the hospital that's thirty miles from her home. It's where she was born and her sister too. We're far away at the moment, but I think of that hospital oh so often.

Nostalgia, perhaps.

When I looked up her birth records years ago, I noted her mother was also born in that hospital, delivered by the same doctor. A woman named Meredith was proud to be the lucky doctor who brought them both into the world. Isn't it a beautiful thing, bringing a new, innocent life into this chaos?

Staring at the monitors while Delilah stares at Cody, I think back on those days, the earliest ones of my life.

There's not much before the barn that I remember. Only the immediate events leading to it. I consider those events my conception. After all, had they never happened, I wouldn't be who I am.

She was born in the hospital and I was born in that barn.

"I appreciate it, Cody, really I do ... but I can't stay here." With her arms crossed, Mr. Walsh should know he's not winning this one. It's his controlling nature, his arrogance even, in thinking his home is better suited than Delilah's.

Turning my head to face the window, I can make out their silhouettes through the curtains. From my vantage point, and given their positions, it's easy to tell they're having a heated argument. Having the monitors, though, is far more helpful. I should feel guilty that a system I put in place years ago is now being exploited. I should feel many things ... and I am, just not the correct emotions.

My phone buzzes with a message, but it's not one from either of them and I'm far too interested in this development.

Their argument is unfortunate. Not because I wish them pleasantness, or because either of the two are making a better case than the other. It's unfortunate simply because the raised voices and harsh tones are so very reminiscent of a lovers' quarrel.

Memories swirl and I lean back against the roof tiles. With the moon setting just beneath the tree line, it's dark enough that no shadows can survive. They'll never see me, but I can see them just fine.

And with the monitor in my hand, I can hear them just as clearly.

The tears that streak down Delilah's face remind me of the first time I went to the hospital that carries so much weight on my conscience this morning.

It was that little girl, with the same tears, who changed my decision. She was there and I didn't expect it. Had the events been different, and her father been the only one brought in with the unconscious woman losing her breath, I'd have told them all. I would have relied on what a former version of me was told to do, before this new one was conceived.

I could have spent hours mourning over every vision and letting it all spill out, but I kept it all in, swallowed it down and watched her being held in the arms of a monster. And she clung to him. Her head was tucked so carefully under his chin while the woman was whisked away on a gurney.

I remember standing there, thinking this very thought: this is where people are born. The stark white walls and the yells of nurses blurred with the wide eyes of a little girl who was scared. I wonder if she would remember. I doubt she does. I remember it all, though.

The thing about that unit is that most of the people I surrounded myself with were born there. I wasn't. I was so far gone from my hometown because I ran north when I should have run south. I know that now, but back then I didn't. I wasn't born in my hometown either, though.

I was birthed in that barn.

With the stench of pigs, and old dirt that felt like clay. The child who ran away, somehow escaping certain death, thought that structure would be a place to heal. But that's all he was, a child who should have died. A child who deserved to die for what he'd done.

So I let him. I let that boy suffer, I forced him to watch and accept what he allowed to happen. I didn't tell anyone what had really occurred and I knew that woman would die.

But the monster was comforting his little girl. How I could I, of all people, take someone's parent away?

The biggest difference between my birth and so many others, is that they came into this world innocent, being held dearly, if screaming wildly. Well ... most of them. The lucky ones.

I became the person I am when I was seeking shelter in that barn from monsters and watching a man who I knew nothing about commit unspeakable acts of horror that haunted every night of that sanctuary.

I suppose it doesn't matter where or how you're born, though ... much less so than where and how you die.

"I'm leaving, Cody." Delilah's voice is raised and it wavers at the end of her statement. The pain she's feeling is etched into his name. *Let her go.* She doesn't need a damn soul comforting her. Least of all his.

"How can you protect me better than anyone else if there's

nothing you know that I don't?" the lawyer in her whips at him and a slow grin crawls into place on my face. She knows he knows, and she can't let it go. That knowledge brings me more peace than it should as I breathe in the crisp fall air.

"Please," he says, pleading with her and his tone is genuinely desperate. I catch the small details of her expression shift. The thin creases around her downturned lips and the way her gaze softens.

Holding my breath, I watch him touch her as if she belongs to him. As if he can hold her and comfort her and make everything all right.

That's not the way it works. He can't make it better. What's worse is that he *knows* he can't.

She's a strong woman, but not strong enough. That's obvious from the way she says his name, like it's the only word she knows.

We all know better. As he leans in and kisses her, her arms wrapping around his shoulders, all I can think is that we all know better.

My phone buzzes again and his messages can't wait any longer. I could stay here and listen to her sweet moans all night ... but then he'd be the one kissing her.

Personal conflicts aside, I'll have to leave this ending to be a surprise.

If people knew the story of how I grew up, they would feel so badly for me. Most of them would. If, however, I started that tale with the barn ... a sarcastic huff leaves me as I picture women securing their arms around their children and slowly backing away.

The metal stairs to the fire escape creak and groan as I climb down until my boots hit the pavement.

The streetlights shine down on me and that's just fine. With the jacket that's tight across my shoulders sporting an electric company logo and the nondescript black bag in my hand, I'm merely out on the job. Fixing a broken cable box or whatever the hell will do the trick to get bystanders feeling comfortable.

I went from being a boy abducted from his shitty hometown with crime rates that rivaled the most dangerous cities, to becoming an onlooker in a sleepy suburb, hiding in an abandoned barn while I observed the most heinous of crimes. I spent my days watching a man who defended both the innocent and guilty for a living, a man everyone seemed to look up to.

It wasn't often he came to the barn with his victims. But my birth was a long one and I learned who I was, what I wanted, and more importantly, how and why I should kill.

I was the lucky one who escaped one hell, only to be birthed into another.

Chapter 3

Delilah

It's far too quiet in this apartment now that I'm alone. It's late and the residents above me, the Whitmores, must have gone to bed early or left for vacation. I haven't heard a thing through the floorboards. It would offer me peace any other time to know the obnoxious pacing and thuds of heavy footsteps are silenced for whatever reason, but not tonight.

I can't help but to focus on the fact that last time I showered here, Marcus brought roses to my kitchen. He broke in and not a soul knew while I was in this very bathroom. I check my bedroom the moment I step out of the shower, wrapped in nothing but a towel, although I hold on to my gun with a tight grip. The lightweight Beretta hasn't left my side since I've come home.

I take careful steps into every room and I truly wish there were some sign of someone else, even if it's only Mrs. and Mr. Whitmore arguing over the television channel and what to watch next.

No one's here. Not a sound can be heard except for my own nervous heartbeat. My apartment is empty, the security system up and running. A click on the keypad to my laptop, open on my kitchen counter, would show any movement at all surrounding the apartment. Of course I see various people coming and going, mostly neighbors and their friends flowing through the locked front door as they're buzzed in.

With the pads of my feet still damp, I vacate the empty kitchen. The perfectly cleaned island counter, lacking anything at all on it, stays in my mind.

Back in the bedroom, I recheck all the windows. It's the back bedroom window that I'm certain Marcus came in through before. I don't have any proof but it would only make sense. It backs up to brush, so it'd be difficult, but it's quiet along that street with hardly anyone there to witness a break-in.

With a prick climbing up my spine, I stare at the window, the gun slipping against my palms until I breathe out a frustrated sigh.

This is necessary. Getting used to being home alone after a break-in is something that simply has to happen. I'm not the only one who goes through this anxiety. There's a break-in nearly every thirteen seconds, adding up to over two and a half million a year. So many people go through this. Still, as I set the gun down on the counter, remove my shower cap and stare at my reflection, I loathe that fear is leading my actions. I suppose the comparison isn't quite the same. Two and a half million people don't encounter serial killers ... or get gifted flowers and forbidden kisses during their break-ins.

My gaze drops to my lips and I let my fingertips drift there. It's not like I'd use the gun, I remind myself as I set it down and go about my routine.

I have questions and Marcus has answers. Answers Cody supposedly doesn't have. Taking my time with my moisturizer and normal nightly routine, I let the accusations toward both Cody and Marcus build up in my mind. Right before shutting them all down again.

My bed creaks when I sit on the edge of it, spreading a sweet-smelling lavender lotion down my thighs and calves. The oversized sleep shirt I'm wearing is a soft cotton and I let myself breathe for a moment. Auntie Susan used to tell me, *You have to give yourself grace; no one else will.*

I can't help the small whisper in response at the back of my mind: *Cody would. Cody would grant me grace.* Hell, letting out my frustration in a huff, I place the amber glass bottle of lotion on my dresser and know that he gave me more grace than he should have this past weekend. I don't deserve it, and he knows that now. Yet he still wanted me and I can't fathom why.

My mind is still a whirlwind of everything that's happened in the past few weeks.

Pretending as if I'll sleep at all tonight, I take the lightweight gun with me to the kitchen for a glass of water to bring to bed. This gun is coming with me everywhere. I have my firearms license and there's not a chance in hell Cody would have let me walk out his door without it. The kitchen light is still on and the front door boasts a blinking red light, signifying the alarms are all set. If anyone were to try to join me tonight in this place, the alarms will sound and Cody will know instantly too.

I'm not blind to the fact that he's circled the building multiple times. In fact, it warms something inside of me.

If anyone had told me years ago that he would look out for me like he has, I'd have told them to fuck off and stop filling my brain with white knight fantasies.

I didn't get to where I am in life by relying on anyone else. Taking another sip of my water, I lean against the farmhouse sink.

This morning, naked in Cody's bed, I came to a simple conclusion. I want to be in my own home and alone. No security detail, no prince in shining armor with a sad backstory. No nothing. I need to be on my own. How am I going to get better if I rely on Cody? I can't and I won't. Given this past weekend, I've obviously lost it.

Half a day on my own has already been good for me and

clearing my head. The first half was spent arguing with Cody ... again. The water rushes out of the faucet and I fill my glass before heading back to my mostly cleaned bedroom.

I spent the rest of the day unpacking and cleaning up the piles of paperwork, all while talking to my sister. We spent nearly three hours on the phone. First, I let her unload and then I did some unloading of my own, keeping out some small details. Like every piece about Marcus. Somehow, he's become my secret and I don't know what will happen if I tell anyone. Really I'm afraid of what will happen if I tell. I'll lose him and quite possibly ostracize myself, lose my job ... forfeit my sanity. No one knows I kissed him, and I'd like to keep it that way.

My phone buzzes on my nightstand, so I trade it for the glass of water and plop down cross-legged on the bed.

Mom is doing better.

I answer my sister quickly enough to hopefully put her anxious mind at ease: *Good. I knew she would.*

I'm still worried. Something's just not right.

I hesitate, not knowing what to tell Cadence until I settle on: *You're a worrier. Mom is fine and she knows she can come to us if she needs anything.*

My fingers reach up to the collar of my throat, to that dip where a thin chain would rest if I was wearing a necklace. It's a nervous habit, but instead of touching metal it's only skin brushing against skin as I assure myself, yes, she would. *Mom would tell us if she needed us. She'd tell us if anything was wrong.*

My message to my sister goes unanswered even though I'm aware she's read it and so I start to doubt myself. Without waiting any longer for her to reply, I promise her I'll be home this weekend and we can have a girls' night. *Just the three of us.*

Her joke about me having time off over a reporter and bad press makes me roll my eyes, but more than that, I'm grateful for the distraction. I shake my head at the thought that all that's wrong right now in my life is just bad press. What a pretty little lie.

The truth will come out and you'll be back to your workaholic self. It's the last text she sends before I plug in my cell and decide I really need to sleep. I've barely slept to the point where now my eyes are raw and dry. I got in a half hour catnap earlier but woke up with my heart beating out of my chest. If I can sleep tonight without waking up in a panic, I'll count it as a win.

No sleeping pills, though; I want to stay alert. No, I think as I sigh heavily, I *need* to stay alert.

The moment I lay down, a satin wrap around my hair and the blanket tucked all the way up to my chin, my phone pings but it's not my sister like I expect.

I'm only a phone call away. Cody's message elicits a guilt that barricades my throat. I have to swallow it down before telling him I know and I'm here if he needs anything.

I add in a *thank you*, although it doesn't offer me any

peace. I shouldn't be thanking him for my independence.

It's not like we're more than fuck buddies and I almost tell him that, but my wretched heart hurts daring to think the words, let alone say them. I don't want anything more, and neither does he that I'm aware of. So all of this ... the protection he's given me ... it's just him being kind and doing what he knows how to do. I appreciate that.

I appreciate you, I write to him because that's all I know how to say right now. It doesn't explain why the back of my eyes prick with unshed tears and I suddenly feel so alone.

Lying on my back and staring at the spinning ceiling fan, I come to the only conclusion my exhausted mind has to offer: I think I'm falling for him and that's terrifying. In all of this mess and turmoil, my heart is apparently in chaos too. Last night, I slipped deeper into his arms than I ever have before.

He's only a phone call away and he's texted me that twice already tonight. That's good enough for now.

I swear I try to sleep. I forced my eyes closed, my bed is warm and cozy ... I even got up around 2:00 a.m. for a drink of chamomile tea that I sucked down as quickly as I could so I didn't have to have my eyes open for too long. All the effort to sleep doesn't work; sleep evades me.

The alarm clock reads nearly 4:00 a.m. as I sit in my bed,

reading through a folder of evidence. If I can't sleep, I can at least work.

Ross Brass is the one case I chose. Even if his charges were dropped, he's a suspect in another case. There are more murders with his signature and now an APB is out. But he's in the wind.

It's the case that makes the most sense for me to look into. With nothing but time on my hands and a stain on my reputation, both because of him, I want this bastard behind bars for more than one reason. It's not a vendetta, though, it's simply my fucking job.

It's not the case that's opened on my laptop laying only a foot from me on the bed. The dim light of it calls to me to come back to it even though I've read through it a dozen times already. There's not much there, to be honest. Twenty years ago, detective work wasn't what it is now. The lack of forensics and technology and protocols ... it all adds up to incomplete files, scanned papers that are more incoherent thoughts and assumptions that aren't backed up than anything else.

What is known is that there were three men, at least, who kidnapped, assaulted and sexually abused a number of boys ranging from six years to ten years old. Two men were found dead at the scene, where the remains of the missing boys were found buried along with evidence that they were fed to the dogs roaming around the property. The third man was badly injured by the dogs; with his throat ripped out, he died in the hospital hours after discovery. One boy was alive when police arrived, only to die shortly after in the care of medical professionals who simply couldn't treat all his injuries.

The case is a horror story and a tragedy that kept mothers awake at night. It destroyed a small town in northeastern New York and I can't even imagine what their families went through.

Including Cody, given that Christopher was only identified by teeth buried in the black dirt and the little boy who survived said he was alive only days before. A week would have made a difference in a life. A single week. The lead detective on the case retired shortly after and one note I haven't forgotten is in the files. A note stating that he suspected one of the men nearly a year before they were caught, but nothing came of the home search.

A photograph stares back at me as I drag the device into my lap and lean against the headboard.

Christopher Walsh was one of the sixteen boys over the course of four years.

There's no one to question now, only ghosts.

Yet questions pile up in my mind, refusing to let it go, because deep down inside I'm vaguely aware there's something here that I'm supposed to know.

The creak of the floor is synonymous with a number of things. The first being a striking fear that runs through me, followed by a chill that rolls down my spine. The second and most obvious is an unsolicited exhale and the memory of the last time I saw Marcus.

His mouth on mine, his body so close I can still feel the heat of him. The detailed reminder that comes with a whisper of his kiss against my lips washes away so much of everything else in this very moment.

Still, my gaze shifts from the darkened corner where a man obviously stands, to my gun, very much in clear sight on my nightstand.

With my pulse both heating and racing, I struggle to move. Another creak of the floorboards shifts the shadow and I stare into the darkness.

"It's only me," he speaks, breaking the silence.

My question is merely a murmur. "Should I close my eyes?" I don't know how I'm able to breathe, let alone whisper the words.

I can't see a damn thing but I swear I know he's smiling when he answers me, his voice gruff as if he hasn't spoken in a long, long time. "It depends on two things."

The thumping in my chest is harder and my body hotter in every way possible, to the point that I desperately need to move out from under the covers, but my body is far too paralyzed to do so.

"What two things?"

"Can you see me?"

A hesitant exhale accompanies the headshake I offer as an answer.

"Good."

"And the second thing?"

"Is that gun for me?"

Lie to him, my inner voice hisses, but the truth comes out instead as I say, "Yes. You or anyone else who broke in ... but I figured it'd be you. How did you get in?"

There's a hint of something in my voice I can't quite place. My gaze follows the slight shift along the dark shadow.

"Because you're scared?" he asks and ignores my questions. A hardness as well as curiosity are present in his tone.

"Yes," I say, offering the word but I'm not sure he heard it so I nod and with it, my arms finally move. Even that small a change seems too much and I do everything I can to be as still as possible.

It feels as if my body is trembling, but when I peer down, I'm still as a statue.

"Don't be afraid. I don't have any desire to hurt you." The recognition of his voice, of the event that transpired in Cody's kitchen loosens my coiled muscles. Again I peer at the gun before turning back to the darkness in the corner. He must be leaning against the wall.

"Does that mean I don't have to close my eyes?" I ask him.

"You really should."

My throat is tight as I swallow and the sound it makes is audible and wretched.

Marcus only chuckles, and then tsk-tsks me. "I said don't

be afraid, Delilah."

"How long have you been here?" I ask him, focusing on my alarm clock that now blinks 12:12 in a harsh red, mocking me. My phone never alerted me that the power went out.

"Maybe a half hour... That seems about right." Gesturing to the blinking clock, the man I believe is dressed in all black, or at least dark colors, only responds, "It had to be fast not to set off the alarm. Don't blame yourself for not noticing right away. You were so caught up in ... a case? I presume?"

I still can't make out his features, but I know he has a hood above his head. Something that could easily block his face if he wished. His outline is defined with broad shoulders and the height of a tall man. Every other detail, though, is hidden from view.

So I keep my eyes open and ask again, "How did you get in?"

"The same as before. Does it matter?" he asks and I shake my head although it feels deceitful. Of course it matters. Every detail matters.

"I have a question for you," I say and the words come out unbidden.

"I have some for you too, want to trade?" Amusement laces his response and I can't ignore the stir in the pit of my belly.

There's a touch of menace in his question but I gather my strength and my sanity, refusing to fall deeper into the hole I've found myself in.

"How did you get in before? The power didn't go out

then." Although the second statement is firm with resolve, the moment it slips from my lips I question its truthfulness.

His tone reflects boredom and that strikes a chord inside of me as he turns his back against the wall, no longer looking at me. Instead he stares at my door and all I'm offered is a silhouette. "I know your security code; I know the brother of a man who was on your security detail who was preoccupied with ... a more pressing matter. Another was busy with a broken light in the parking lot. Distractions. I get in with distractions and contacts and information that's easily traded."

With his tired and clearly disappointed response, he inhales deeply and I ask another question, some mundane part of me still stuck on the *how* or possibly not yet willing to dare ask about the *why*.

"Who told you the code?"

With another tsk he reprimands me, much more seemingly entertained. It's then that I find I've repositioned myself to face him squarely. With his head still firm against the far wall of my bedroom, he turns to look at me and for a moment, I see an outline of his face.

The way he turned and a hint of light from a passing car down the back alley behind my apartment aid me in the moment.

There are details of plump lips and a sharp jawline. Not the hideous face of a killer I once placed on him years ago. I dare to think that he's handsome even. But just as quickly as the light fell on his face, it's gone.

"I have a question for you first." A hum of what could be laughter is caught between his lips as he straightens to ask me, "Why didn't you tell him?"

"Tell who?"

"I don't want to play games, Delilah. The kiss." The singular word is hissed although there's no anger that lingers. Not even a threat lays on the word, yet it sounds worse than sinful. "You didn't tell Cody about our ... moment."

"I—" It's a struggle to identify why, caught in his gaze I can't decipher. The moment after between Cody and I ... I should have, but I lied. "I didn't want to upset him."

"It's not because you're ashamed?" he asks.

"Maybe partly," I say and the heat of anxiety dances along my skin with the admission. It doesn't escape me that this man could do awful things to me if only he wanted, and yet again, I find myself glancing at the gun. I'm dealing with a sociopath; at least that's what his profile determined years ago. I'm well aware of the risks. A smidgen of fear trickles down my spine at the thought of disappointing him ... but I imagine it would be much worse if I lied. Something in my gut refuses to let go of that hunch.

It's Marcus's sudden movement that prevents me from lingering on the horrid possibilities. With an easy stride he takes up residence by my vanity in a tufted chair that's far too small for him. It's almost like a throne he's outgrown.

"It's been a long day and I'm sure you have more ... interesting questions than the last one you asked?"

His statement lingers in the warm night air as the heater kicks on and I can't remember what I asked him last, only that my first question bored him. "I'll give you one more question. Only one. Do you still want to know how I knew the code? Or is there something else burning inside you'd rather have answered?"

His posture isn't expectant as he waits for me, but it's in this moment I decide to take advantage of the opportunity to ask him what pricks at the farthest spot of my consciousness. The article about Cody's brother and the other boys that would still light up on my laptop screen if only I brought it to life will haunt me if I don't ask.

"Do you know about ..." Hesitation wraps itself around me and I have to clear my throat before continuing, "What do you know about Christopher Walsh or the other boy who died ... the one named Marcus?"

"Hearing that name ..." His tone is dampened with sadness. "I know everything about it. More than any one person should. I know the men didn't suffer enough. They never do, though? Do they? It's not about them suffering." He adds the last bit almost as if it's a reminder for himself. "It's about ending what they're capable of."

"You were there?" All the questions I want answered could fill a vault and I edge against the warmth of the comforter, closer to his now hunched figure. But all that anticipation is quickly put out like the flame of an extinguished candle.

"That's another question."

"Please," I beg him out of instinct, my fingers gripping the comforter tightly with the single word. Marcus's head rises ever so slowly and a pale, pale blue stares back at me. The case matters. I knew it did. Other questions scream in my mind. *What about Cody? How much does he know?* They line up one by one, held back only by biting the inside of my cheek.

He's my witness, my ghost. But this isn't a courtroom, a cell or an interrogation. I don't have an ounce of power here and I'm left at his mercy.

The small voice that's been reckless and foolish reminds me of the kiss we shared and my gaze drops to his lips. It reminds me that he came to me. There's a small bit of power in my grasp, but just like every other fact I've uncovered, I don't know why. "I just ..." It takes great effort to lean back in my bed and its groan of protest doesn't stop me from a plan that's more than likely foolish. "How do you know Cody? You know him, don't you?"

"He thinks I'm someone I'm not. He wants me to be that person." Marcus's swallow and exhale reveal the cues of a man struggling. But also a man who's dying to confess. I can be his priest, his doctor, his executioner ... whatever he wants, so long as I'm given that confession. I want it more than I've wanted anything else in a long damn time.

"I'm not that person, but he keeps my secrets and pretends.

And together, we've done so well. We both lost someone at the same time in our lives. I think it's really the bonding that binds us together more than anything. It's the loss."

The cryptic words don't tell me everything, but they tell me enough to know Cody lied. He lied to me. He's keeping Marcus's secrets … or at least that's what this man believes. "What about—"

"Stop," he commands with an authority that's frightening. One not to be denied. "Shhh." He's quick to add the gentleness to his voice when he shushes me, but it's far too late to prevent fear from pressing my back firm against the headboard. "I gave you another question because I have one of my own."

"Yes?"

"Did you like it when I kissed you?" he asks, repositioning himself in the chair, leaning forward so his forearms rest on his thighs as he stares at me through the dark.

The rush of my blood in my ears nearly drowns out every other sense.

Logically, I should tell him yes to appease his ego, his need for control. I've been trained on how to deal with personalities such as his. Although, this is much, much different from any scenario I've confronted in the past. The reality, the truth of his question … it's still a yes. Even as scared as I am, there's a spark that crackles between us. Knowing what he's capable of and yet how soft he has been with me draws me to him for reasons I can't explain.

"Yes," I say and take a deep breath.

"Another trade?" he asks me and before I can stop myself, I answer yes. More than any other reason, it's because I don't want him to leave without knowing more. *I need to know what happened.*

"A touch for a touch?" he says and my eyes widen at the offer. "I didn't let you last time and that seems ... selfish of me."

I can't help the innate fear I feel. The idea of him getting closer to me, close enough to touch, to kiss, all while I stay buried in my bedsheets is both erotic and terrifying.

I know he must see it; I'd be a fool to think I could hide it. Hell, my heart beats so hard, he'd have to be deaf not to hear it staggering with dread. "I'll sweeten the deal. I'll tell you how I know your code. I'll tell you now, if you want."

My gaze peers deeper into his, and I find myself wishing for more light. His desperation is ... not understood. He shouldn't want me, but he does. I can sense it; his desire caresses every inch of me, preparing me for him.

Marcus wants me and I'm ashamed to admit what that knowledge does to me.

Met with silence for too long, Marcus continues. "I have small cameras on the outside of your building. I can watch who comes and goes and more importantly, I can see you put in the code, Delilah. And anyone else I want."

"That's not true. I searched the place down myself."

With a huff of laughter, he leans back in the chair and

responds, "They look like nailheads, so small, and everywhere I want them to be." The arrogance doesn't go unnoticed.

"How long?"

"How long have I been watching you? You have so many questions that you already know the answers to, don't you?"

His taunt prompts me to remember the first week I moved in when there was a day when the power went out. There wasn't an ounce of me that suspected anything. That was years ago ... Years. The answer sends goosebumps down my shoulders that don't stop until a shiver takes over.

"I have unusual ways, invasive, I know. But I tried to stay away and let you be. This is how I managed. And then ... you kissed him. You fucked him. It ... it's taking a lot of effort to not be jealous. He's been there for you and you've seen what he's done for you. It makes sense. You haven't seen what I've done for you, though."

I can barely breathe listening to him.

His jealousy is a shock. And given all this new information, my body trembles. "You told me not to be scared, but I am." I admit the truth out loud because it's too much. It's far too real.

"You're a good girl for telling me." *Good girl.* From anyone else, I would snap at those words. There's a trigger inside of me wound tight and it would spring free. But from him ...

He adds, "We're going to have to work on that. Lie down and let me help you."

"What do you want?" I ask and my voice shakes.

"Again ... You already know the answer."

He's not wrong. I know what he wants; even my body is aware as my nipples harden against the soft cotton of my sleep shirt.

As if he's read my mind, his nearly silver gaze drops to my chest. "Fear is a funny thing, isn't it?" he comments but remains where he is. "I bet you're hot too, aren't you?"

All I can think about is Cody. Marcus may know things, but Cody may not. And whatever I do here, could come back on a man who has done nothing but protect me.

"Marcus ... I'm with—"

"I know. I saw it all. I saw you kiss him again yesterday. Really kiss him like you love him. You do, don't you?" There's not an ounce of anger in his voice, only knowing.

"Marcus—"

"I'm not mad. You don't have to be afraid. But I deserve a chance. I don't regret much in life, but I regret not taking you when I had the chance."

"When was that?" I ask only to allow more time to pass. To give space to the moment so I can think.

"Questions. So many questions, my Delilah." Sitting straighter, his fingers wrap around the arms of the chair as if he's holding himself back. "I answered you, I gave you more information than I should."

"You told me not to be scared, but—"

"If you'd like, I can make it easier on you."

I can only nod.

"Lie down, Delilah." With trembling limbs I slowly do as he says, lifting the covers for a moment, glancing at the gun that's still within reach and knowing it was never going to protect me against Marcus. He takes his time giving me orders, and all the while I listen obediently.

"Close your eyes," he whispers and they're the most seductive words I've ever heard. If only sinning with your eyes closed saved your soul from the devil.

Every little hair stands on edge when I hear the telltale creak of him rising from the chair. My chest rises and falls chaotically, every fight-or-flight instinct within me screaming with pure adrenaline.

"Don't turn around," he commands and I'm certain his steps are deliberately loud as he rounds the bed, walking behind me. Ever so slowly, the weight of him is felt when the cool air from a raised comforter kisses my skin.

With my eyes closed tight, he climbs in behind me and I have to part my lips to inhale. It's a shaky breath that's suffocated in his heat as he gets closer, inch by inch, until his hard chest is nearly against my back. With every breath, I barely graze him. With one more adjustment, his erection presses against my ass. A whimper leaves me and it's then I feel his shadow weighing down on me. His fingers slip a strand of loose hair down my shoulder and he whispers along the curve of my neck.

"He likes to kiss you here ... I understand the desire."

Chapter 4

Marcus

I'm ever so careful with my little mouse. The corners of my lips tug up at the nickname that's been buried so long in my conscious. It's been a lifetime since I thought of her like that. Which is quite different from what I imagine she's thinking right now.

Her shyness and timidness are ... more appealing than I ever dreamed. Although my illicit fantasies that included playing games didn't hold an ounce of wavering. Not on her part and certainly not on mine.

"Touch for a touch, little mouse," I whisper and let the promise ... or threat ... linger before I add, "I go first this time."

The hitch in her breath is accompanied by her eyes shutting tight. The light lays there on the delicate hollow at her throat and unlike what I planned, I graze my teeth along her slender neck, noting how her back arches and her heartbeat pounds. My bottom lip tips just slightly before lifting away, leaving a small bit of moisture just beneath the tender side of her ear.

I can't resist blowing ever so slightly and my reward is a sudden, sharp intake of breath.

"Your turn," I tell her, but she's still for far too long. Doesn't she know what she does to me? How everything twists with her around. Black and white bleed together and all that remains are gray blurs, bringing only her into sharp focus.

"Whatever you want," I say, practically pleading with her as I drop my lips to the shell of her ear. "Take it, ask it, do as you please." Everything about her threatens to make me lose control.

"A question," she says and the words rush out of her. "A touch for a question."

Disappointment is a heavy weight, but I should know better than to push her too soon. My scared little mouse.

"My touch, your question," I respond although I don't agree.

"What do you want after?" she asks and I smirk, my lips grazing her ear as I admonish her, saying, "So expectant."

Goosebumps flow down her caramel skin and I'm eager to touch, lick, and cover them in every way I've dreamt. "After what?" I practically dare her to say it.

Her bottom lip quivers ever so slightly and those long

lashes stay down, covering her gaze I'm desperate to see.

She doesn't answer even though her lips part. I have mercy on her. She deserves that at the very least.

"Don't be afraid. No matter how much I want to fuck you, I won't until you beg me."

I hate how her body relaxes even if she doesn't do it purposefully. It's a tangible sense of relief and that tells me many things. For one, she thought I would take from her. Pressing my hand against her lower belly, my fingers would play along the seams of her panties if the shirt wasn't in my way. I push her back to my front and make sure she feels how hard I am for her before telling her, "Your body may want me now, but you'll be begging me to fuck you, Delilah. You will feel deprived without me inside of you."

A huff of amusement leaves me as the sound slipping from her lips mimics both a moan of pleasure and tortured agony.

"Another question?" I ask her. "My next touch will be lower."

With my warning lingering, she surprises me. Lifting her arm slowly and whispering, so low it's almost not audible, "A touch." Although her eyes stay closed and her body remains as it is, her arm moves behind her head and then behind mine.

Closing my eyes, I let her press her palm against my neck, certain the rough stubble will grate along her soft skin. Her fingers linger there, feeling every inch of the back of my neck and then move higher, up my jaw. When she trails them to my lips, I can't resist the urge to nip them.

Shock ignites within her and she rips her hand away, her eyes opening for just a moment. A moment where perhaps she felt the danger once again.

She'll learn, she'll grow to be at ease around me. I'll make sure of that.

With her breathing erratic still, she forces her eyes closed and I make my next move obvious. Slipping my left hand under the thin fabric of her sleep shirt, I slide all the way up to where it was just a moment ago and then lower, lower still, slipping beneath the elastic of her panties until her pubic hair rests against my fingertips. She's hot, every inch of her, but I'm more than aware that just a bit lower will greet me with a warmth that already has my cock leaking precum.

"Another move on your end?" I whisper softly, daringly. "Question?" I whisper against her hair. "Or touch?" I let the tip of my nose touch her, acutely aware that it breaks the rules, but not giving enough of a damn to stop myself.

It takes every ounce of effort not to turn her onto her belly and take her how she wants to be taken. The way I imagine it is raw and deep. Far too tempting for my lack of patience right now. I allow myself the small nudge of my nose against her neck.

Her swallow is slow, her words even slower. "If I ask you for a time and place, would you agree to only seeing me then?" she asks and what a waste of a question it is.

"No." I answer her with honesty as I slip my fingers lower, drifting them to her slit and bringing her arousal to her swollen nub to rub gentle circles. Her back presses against my chest and her neck arches, bringing her chin closer to my lips when I admit, "I'll see you whenever the fuck I want."

I don't stop the heavy petting, loving her ass pressed back against my sweatpants. Just the feel of her writhing against me forces an aching need to override my senses. Her body tightens and I still, not wanting to send her over the edge just yet. "Another question?" I dare to ask and I do something I haven't in a long damn time. I pray. I pray she has one more so I can press my fingers deep inside her cunt and feel just how tight and hot she is.

"If I message you to come to me, can I see you whenever the fuck I want?"

I hope she can feel my smile against her heated skin as I whisper something I've heard her say a thousand times when she's well aware the answer is no. "We'll see." I wish I could. I wish it were that easy.

With the rest of my answer unspoken, I thrust two fingers inside of her heat, curling them and stroking along the front wall of her pussy while my thumb still presses against her clit. I'm meticulous, drawing it out and memorizing every detail of how her body reacts to the pleasure. Her fingers dig into the covers while her plump lips part and as much as I want to take them with my own, rules are rules. One touch is all she gets.

"Marcus," she says, mewling my name. That's how she comes undone. With me inside of her and my name on her lips.

My last commands to her, which she willingly obeyed: *Stay very still. Close your eyes now. And sleep.*

Chapter 5

Marcus

The bad men always lose.

The boy told me that. I truly believed him back then. I can even remember nodding my head in agreement.

They will lose. They always lose. I look back on it now and know it was the heroes that led us to believe that. Comic drawings depicting superpowers and cartoon shows that came on every morning on the weekends. Even if it was naïve, it's still true. I'll be damned to admit anything else.

The bad men will always lose.

His large eyes stared back at me from across the cell. He said it like it was a question; after all, I was older by almost a year than him and taller too.

"Yeah," I told him, my voice scratchy from lack of water.

"They always lose." I think the entire time we were there together, I barely spoke. Those may have been the first words I uttered out loud besides my name. Because he needed to hear it, and deep down inside I needed to hear it too.

He was the one who did the talking. All his stories kept us going.

The boy said that first night, sometimes they win, and that's what makes them bad guys. Everyone has bad thoughts, but they have to act on them ... for someone to truly be bad. He went on and on, but I didn't respond or agree with that ideology. The boy weaved a story, while I sat against the cold broken stone of reality and let him.

It was only months later when I decided the man who came into the barn every so often with a victim of his own was a bad man. He didn't prey on little boys like the ones in the cell did, but those women were victims nonetheless.

The first time in the barn, my safe haven and escape, I was shocked and sat in horror because it couldn't possibly be happening. Not again. The second time, I crawled out and tried to wake the woman the moment the barn closed with that eerie creak from rusted old hinges. I shook her, I did everything I could to get her to move. That's when I realized I was too late.

What a weak being I was, to shy away until it was too late. Yet that was who I was at my core. It's what defined me. Both the boy and the woman showed me that. Her blond hair was matted with dirty blood when I realized how lacking I was in morality. Hiding to protect myself while allowing others to perish disgusted me, but that's what I did.

I didn't know if the woman was innocent, but the boy was and that's when I heard his voice again: The bad men always lose. Wasn't it bad that I didn't do the right thing? That I wasn't the hero he'd told stories about. I was nothing like the person he thought I was.

And so I waited and I watched because I wanted the bad man to fall. I thought maybe it would make it right. It would make sense, all of the tragedy would, if only I aided in this man's demise.

So I waited, I followed, I watched and planned a way to help the good guys bring him down ... because back then, I thought there were heroes who wanted to take down men like him. I thought they would listen and they'd bring the monsters to justice.

It didn't take long before I realized no one would come. They came after me instead. They wouldn't listen to what I was saying. I was a dirty, lost kid and all they wanted to know was my name. They didn't listen to me. And I couldn't bring myself to say my name. They couldn't take me away. Not when I had so much work to do to make up for the bad things I'd allowed to happen.

I decided I had to be the one. I'd be the reason that bad man would lose.

It would be justice for the boy. All of the bad men need to pay and it started with him.

I hadn't counted on her sneaking in, her hair in wild curls and the smile on her face so pure and full of hope. It had been so long since I'd seen a smile like that. Shock held me in place as the screwdriver in my hand, the longest one I could find in the abandoned place, slipped to the floor. He would have heard; she would have been my undoing if not for her shriek of laughter hiding the dull bang.

What was that sound doing in this place? It didn't belong here. She didn't belong here either.

She called him Daddy and ran to him while he cleaned his hands with the same towel that had blood on it not too long ago.

Through the broken wood slat I watched, the weapon at my feet in the hay that I was certain now smelled more like me than I reeked of it.

Conflict took ahold of me for the first time in a long time. I wasn't sure what to do and the boy's voice was quiet. I think he would have liked her too.

The man was a monster, but I watched him hold her hand.

I followed from a distance, safe enough to see it all.

The man was bad, that I knew. And he would lose; I knew that too.

My small child's mind was uncertain where she fit in and where I fit in. Until I came up with another plan, one the boy loved even more.

He can teach me how to kill. He does it so well.

I'll let the one bad man live for a while. After all, I needed someone to teach me. Who best to learn from than the monster himself? And I couldn't be the reason the girl stopped smiling. I couldn't take her father away, not when I knew how much pain it would cause.

Sitting back in the worn leather seat of the marked van, I watch the series of text messages on my laptop. They're not to me, but they certainly hold my interest.

Everything about her holds my interest these days. I've been watching and waiting, not so differently than what I've done for years, but for far different reasons.

The dim light of the evening approaches and I'm aware that the residents of this friendly neighborhood will find their way back to their two-story homes on this quiet street. I'll wave and smile as they pass by in their large SUVs and family vans with little stick figures of their children on the back windows. And they'll do the same, smiling and waving back. I've been told I should have been a dentist because of my smile. Not the electrician I'm pretending to be.

Another message pings on my screen and a shred of jealousy seeps into my blood. I don't recall experiencing the feeling as much as I have recently. Even back then, when she loved the monster and didn't even know I existed.

Years passed and there was never a time that I was jealous. Even as I played with the strings bringing Delilah and Cody closer together. I couldn't be with her, not when I had so much work to do to make up for the mess I allowed as I learned. I had so much to make amends for. But then he kissed her.

And she kissed him back.

I know she wanted him to for a long while. She wanted his lips on hers. She wanted more than that.

I imagine tonight he'll lean in for a kiss but I'm uncertain if she'll allow it. Since I kissed her last. I wonder which kiss she enjoys more.

Honk, honk, the man I saw just a moment ago waves me down from the other side of the street. He's heading the other direction now, the front end of his car parallel to mine and his window rolled down.

With jet-black hair speckled white and wrinkles lining his eyes, he narrows his gaze at me, a harsh crease in his forehead emphasizing his wrinkles.

A smirk is my response as he motions for me to roll down my window. I do and immediately ask him, "You lost?"

"No, no, I thought you might be?" he says with a half grin but skepticism still lingering in his gaze. I've dealt with many men like him, so not an ounce of nervousness trickles through. They're all the same.

I imagine he's retired, the grandfather of one of the youths who play in these fenced-in backyards. I wonder if he thinks he knows everyone on this street. Maybe he does.

"Not lost," I say as I shake my head and switch the tab on my screen to the work order scheduled at 47 Lewisville Drive. "I'm just waiting on the Jenkinses for their appointment."

The Jenkins family has an appointment, but not with me. Before they arrive, I'll be gone. I'm not interested in their home in the least. This street, however, is one of my favorites for the view I needed tonight. From this exact spot, I can easily see through the back windows of the Italian restaurant a mile down the road, using the camera in my dashboard. Technology has made what I do substantially easier to keep tabs on certain men.

This man is right to be suspicious, but this street will never be harmed. It's far too valuable to me.

"I'm hoping they'll be home soon although I'm early. I got done with my last appointment a little early and …" I don't finish the statement; instead I hold up a half-eaten sandwich.

"Right, right," he says and the grin on his face widens, acknowledging my lies with understanding. He seems to be a good man. One who'd fill me in if ever I needed to know anything about this street. I wouldn't even have to pry for him to confide in me. Men like him are proud to keep an eye out and protect the neighborhood. They're the ones who take it the hardest when something … unfortunate occurs.

I call men like him the birds. They watch, they swoop down to be heroes, but they are so limited when it comes to putting down the dogs.

It's only once the man, who told me his name is Dave, has driven off do I click over to my tabs on the laptop. First checking the cameras and waiting for Ross Brass to make his entrance. He's a no-show at the moment, but given who he's meeting, I'm certain he'll arrive any moment now.

In the meantime, I read the texts between Cody and Delilah.

I need to see you. Cody's been relentless. I can't blame him. He's worried and for good reason. I haven't responded to the messages he's sent me. I'm sure that's caused some unfortunate thoughts to enter his mind.

I never thought I'd hear you say that. I can practically hear her voice hum the somewhat flirtatious response.

Please, tonight.

It must be more than jealousy that I feel when she gives in. Perhaps ... it's obsession. Although from what I know of that shortcoming, it often comes with anger. And there's not a bit of it at the thought of her loving Cody. She has such a big heart. I've seen her love a monster before. She could love me too. I know she can. But it would be so much easier to love Cody.

The faint sounds of chairs scraping and men with thick accents greeting each other force me to click over to the other screen. It's already recording but still, I watch and wait. These strings are more important to pull than the ones of lovers.

Chapter 6

Delilah

It's easier to pretend like it didn't happen than to face the reality. Every other minute, those piercing blue eyes penetrate my every thought and remind me that I saw him again, kissed him again, and was dying for it like I had before. Not only that, but so much more transpired.

And I enjoyed it. I wanted more.

I could lie like an expert witness on the stand and tell myself it was for answers, but the crackle I felt between us, the dose of lust and shot of heat can't be ignored. There's something fucked up in my head. It's wrong and I'm aware, but I can't change it, no matter how much I lie to myself.

Shutting off the blinker puts an end to the clicking as I park my car in the parking lot. My motions are automatic as I reach for both the umbrella and my purse before stepping out onto the wet asphalt. There's only a bit of rain spitting from the skies, but with my hair newly done, I'm not risking a drop landing anywhere near me.

The whoosh and click of the umbrella opening amid the staccato of my heels is followed by my car door shutting as I search for Cody's car.

A coffee date with my FBI agent lover two days after I came apart in my bed at the hands of a serial killer, I would imagine, is unique for the patrons of this diner.

It's a cute place with cozy seating, located at the corner of a quaint street on the far end of town. Even the pastel blue sign that reads Pick Me Ups in a flowing script is adorable. It doesn't fit the man I'm meeting or the relationship we have. Coffee is coffee, though, and this is far more casual than the dinner date he preferred and I turned down.

The second I spot Cody's car, I know I should quicken my pace to get to him. I already told him I was running late, and I hate to keep him waiting. My limbs betrays me, though, and the thumping in my chest refuses to support my body's need to move.

It's almost like this moment is the same as the other night. I'm participating, but not really here. There's space between and I'm merely observing.

The flesh and bones of my body are present and yet I'm only the shadow. Oh how easy it would be, if one could slink away and hide from reality that easily. But as I approach the black glass front doors and shake out the umbrella on the thick black welcome mat out front, I know all too well that I did what I did.

I just don't know what Cody's done, what he knows, or what I'm willing to tell him.

There's more than what he's willing to tell. Between coffee and small talk about scandal and murderers threatening me, I have to decide where Cody fits into all of this with far too limited information.

The door swings open and warmth hits my face while the delectable scent of coffee and citrus pastries swarms my lungs.

Black and white checkered floors, subway tiles and a long coffee bar with black leather stools give the place charm and a '50s flair.

I didn't even want to see his handsome face. I didn't want those steely blue eyes to see right through me, but in this moment, when Cody's gaze locks onto mine from a booth in the back corner, I feel weak. Drawn to him and eager to tell him everything. Literally, I'm desperate to tell him everything.

To expose every little detail. The desire passes as quickly as it came.

"Would you like me to take that for you?" a waitress with coral pink lipstick asks and smiles at me. As I hand over the umbrella and my coat, my pulse quickens. Cody's gaze is still on me, but I can't look back at him.

I'm second-guessing everything. Every move. Every piece of the puzzle. With a heavy exhale I take the seat across from Cody and offer him a simper.

"Still in one piece," he comments and with it I broaden my smile, which makes him smile in return. It's always struck me as such a charming smile. "You had me worried," he says.

Although I part my lips as if I have an easy response to give him, which I don't, I'm saved by the waitress. The same one who took my coat in her poofy dress with puffed sleeves and a black apron tied at her waist.

"A hot cup of coffee is exactly what I need, please."

"Flavor of the day is blueberry."

"Just regular, please." She nods and turns to Cody.

"Black for me." The waitress blushes at Cody's response, as if he's just hit on her by ordering coffee.

"Not sleeping well?" he asks when she slips off.

I shake my head no, although that's not quite true. I'm sleeping better now than I was at his place. It seems unnecessary to tell him that, though.

"You could always come back," Cody says and the guilt weighs down on me at the offer. When did the tables turn between us? With him pining for me while I keep my distance?

The truth nearly slips out from between my lips as my heart aches inside my chest, moaning something to my lungs about how much we need him. I wouldn't be able to forgive myself if something happened to him. That's the one truth that hasn't faltered. That and the fact that I'm certain something bad is going to happen.

When you play with fire, you're bound to be burned. I refuse to let him be a bystander in the wreckage I'm headed toward. Thankfully I don't have to answer, since the waitress is back in no time with our coffee.

We're quiet, neither of us speaking until she asks us if there's anything we'd like to eat.

"Cinnamon buns," we answer simultaneously. The smile I wear on my face at that is a sad one and Cody sees it.

"So ... about my place versus yours?"

Swallowing thickly, I carefully pick up the simple mug of coffee and take a sip before giving him an answer he should accept.

"I'm not sure if you remember, but I wasn't sleeping well at your place either and I like being on my own."

Images blur together in my mind. The memory of Cody's broad chest above mine as he thrust himself inside of me, mixes with the sharp intake I took as Marcus pressed himself against me.

The sudden onslaught of detailed debauchery has me nearly dropping the white ceramic mug on the saucer. It clanks in protest and with trembling hands, I cover my eyes. Vaguely, Cody's apology is little more than white noise.

"Sorry," he says but I'm quick to object to it.

"No, I'm sorry. You don't need to apologize."

"Are you sure you're okay?" he asks and all I can think of saying in response is a lie.

"I told you. I'm tired." I'm not, though. I cling to my coffee cup. This is how cheaters must feel. This wretched twisting in my gut roils and churns. We didn't have a label, we didn't have rules or boundaries. Nevertheless, we have secrets.

It was odd before, between us. But caught in Cody's gaze, it's almost torturous now. I sit across from a man whose only personal possessions are those of a boy he lost long ago. And I know Marcus knew his brother. What I don't know is if Cody knows it too.

Without trust, the tension is palpable as I pick up the bun the waitress sets down, the one I'm certain I won't be able to stomach.

"Thank you for coming. I know after the other night ..." he doesn't finish his trailing thought.

"I'm sorry." The apologies don't quit and for once, I don't mind it. Because I am so damn sorry. Truly to the pit of my stomach. Every definition of the word.

"You don't need to be sorry; I just need to know what's going on," he says, emphasizing the last bit.

"What do you mean?"

"It's been days, Delilah."

"Very uneventful days," I say but stare at the pastry. "You aren't my keeper, Cody. You don't have any responsibility to protect me."

"What if I want to?" he asks.

With a slow inhale, I stare back at him and note the darkness under his eyes and the way his right hand rests palm up on the table. As if it's waiting to be held.

"Any more letters?" he asks and I shake my head easily.

"No letters." I decide to give him all of the truth from yesterday, but none from the night before. "I kept the monitor and the gun right beside me all day and didn't leave my place."

"And nothing?" he questions further, his brow knitting.

"My ass is flat and sore from the way I sat in bed, but no, nothing to report." I hate the way the lie comes so easily.

"Do you remember the letter from the cases we were on in the beginning?" I ask him, treading into the murky waters with so many unanswered questions. "The ones the article mentioned from that bitch reporter who first got me suspended?"

Cody's posture changes instantly. He remembers. We both know he does and unlike what I've been doing, he doesn't lie to me. "Yeah. I remember."

"One of the last FBI task force meetings ... do you remember how I had to walk away for a moment?"

"The crime scene photos were awful," he says and I nod, remembering how the graphic pictures of the victims nearly made me vomit on the spot and I walked off to be alone.

"Right, but it wasn't because I got sick ... I was crying. It was too much, the way the bodies ..."

I can't even begin to think of how he'd left them like that. Cody agrees, "It was brutal."

"I swore I felt someone watching me back there when I stepped outside to get away from it all." I dare to confess something I haven't before when I add, "I thought it was you. I thought you followed me out ... but now I wonder if it was him."

An anonymous tip was left at the station later that night. "He said he'd stop and he did."

"Yeah." Cody nods in agreement and remembrance. "They couldn't find anything on the note. No prints or residue. But they matched the handwriting."

"After that the case went cold."

"I remember. It was like he vanished. We knew he hadn't, though."

"So many cases went cold," I say, recalling them all. All the faces of the deceased. It helps that Jill Tucker from the local eleven o'clock news happened to list them all not too long ago.

"We didn't have the evidence we needed." Cody gives the same excuse the DA gave. Evidence. It doesn't matter what happened. All that matters is what we can prove.

"We knew, though," he says.

"Yeah ... we knew."

When did he start keeping secrets for Marcus? The question echoes in my mind. I wonder if it was then. I swear I felt someone watching me then. It had to have been Marcus.

"I know I asked you before …" I trail off as nerves creep up, weakening my voice and I wish I could take it back, but I can't. Instead I clear my throat and reach for the dewy glass for a quick sip of water instead of coffee. The cold beads of condensation on the side of the glass make it slip in my unsteady grasp.

"I asked you if there was anything you knew about Marcus that I didn't," I remind him and my nails press into the pads of my fingers as I anxiously fidget under the table. Marcus said Cody keeps his secrets. What secrets would he keep from me? Are they about the case? Cases that may get me disbarred if that reporter has her way. Or is it all about his brother. "If there was anything at all that you knew."

"You did," he says and I can see there's more on the tip of his tongue but he swallows it. It wouldn't have been a revelation. Judging by the look of condemnation on his face, it was an accusation. Probably something to the effect of, *after you searched through a box of my dead brother's belongings*. He wouldn't do that to me, though. He wouldn't throw it in my face. That's not the kind of man Cody is.

I wish he would. I wish he'd give me a reason to throw the truth at him just the same.

"You'd tell me, wouldn't you?" I ask him cautiously, reminding myself of the history we have together and the grace and protection he's given me. "Even if you had secrets with Marcus?" My words are barely audible.

They hang in the space between us, joined by the flashes of memories that dance with shadows and illicit thoughts you're only ever supposed to dream about, not live.

The waitress comes by with a smile but it vanishes when she pauses at our table, the tension palpable. "I'll leave you to it," she murmurs and taps the table. "If there's anything you need, you just let me know."

With nods from each of us, she's gone.

"Even if you had secrets with Marcus, you'd tell me, wouldn't you?" I question him again, unwilling to give it up, and his response determines my next move.

"Of course I would," he answers and then sips his coffee, but his voice is flat and so is the thud in my chest.

Like it's given up.

It's wrong, so wrong. Something is badly fucked up in my head knowing that I trust a beast like Marcus over Cody Walsh.

"I'm going to see my sister this weekend," I say to change the subject. "And my mother."

Cody only nods and the silence prolongs itself. There's only the chatter of other patrons and a ding at the door when someone leaves.

"Did something change?" Cody asks with a hint of pain in his tone.

"It does feel different, doesn't it?" I respond with my own question, my walls up and solid as stone.

"I don't know," he says then shakes his head and huffs,

his thumb tapping on the side of the mug in front of him. "I don't know if you'd even let me kiss you right now."

Tink, tink, it's the sound of a lifeline. The moment slowing between us and I'm so very aware that I'm the one left to make the deciding factor.

There's one reason why I lean in and kiss the man who I'm certain is lying right to my face, as I'm doing to him.

It's because I want to, because I love him. And more than anything I want him to know that he is loved. Even if we are lying to each other.

I want to pretend it's only the shadow of a kiss, and that it will stay there on the black and white penny tile of a coffee shop, where our story can change with every new couple who sits in these seats. But it's not. It's the bittersweet, sad kind of kiss, the one where you don't want to move away because it feels so final if you do move.

His lips are soft and his hand cups the side of my head, holding me there. I'm grateful for that, for all of it.

Everything up to this moment has felt like a lie, everything but this kiss and the next words spoke.

With his forehead resting against mine, he inhales in relief but exhales slower.

"You know I'll keep you safe. You know I care about you, don't you?" With his question spoken, his eyes peer into mine and he pulls back.

He pulls back in that way that makes me want to move

closer to him.

"I do." *I really, really do.* "You know I'd do the same, right?" I ask him.

"You don't have to, though."

It's a sad smile that plays quietly on my lips. That's the only response I can give him.

Chapter 7

Delilah

The numbers on the digital display climb and climb while the smell of gasoline lingers. The wet spots on the cracked asphalt prove whoever was at pump three before me left droplets right where I'm standing.

Leaning against my car, I glance up at the lone vehicle that drives down the small-town road this gas station resides on and then check my phone again. It's an old town and just across the street are houses long overdue for renovations. I couldn't imagine living there. Maybe a long time ago it wasn't like it is now. Some other time a lifetime ago.

With a deep inhale, I turn my attention back to my own problems and my own life. Or rather my cell phone.

Two messages. Two different numbers. Two very

different men.

Marcus: *You haven't told Cody about it. But you also haven't messaged me.*

For a woman with such a curious mind ... I expected you would message me.

Cody: *Call me when you get there. I need you to keep me updated.*

Both men have expectations. Yet I have no idea what I can truly expect from either of them. Cody swears he has a lead on a case that'll put him only twenty minutes from the hotel I stay at when I visit home. He lies. He lies to me shamelessly and now that I know that, I see him so differently.

Marcus sent a small bouquet of pink roses before I left. I thought of bringing them along to give to my sister or mother, just to get them out of the house. There was no note, no name, just a small bouquet of the palest pink roses. Their stems were cut down to only six inches or so and the half dozen sat in a square glass vase. I left them there, though, on the kitchen island where the last bouquet sat.

Two men. Twice as many expectations.

I leave both messages alone, not texting either of them back.

After less than a minute passes, my phone buzzes with another text. The nervous butterflies in my stomach settle when I glance down and see it's only my sister, telling me to drive to our mom's instead of her place and that she'll be there a bit later. She had an emergency session come up.

It's easy to respond to her. Although if my life were any semblance of normal, maybe I'd feel the anxiety of my previous visit.

The memories of the bruises flash back, complete with my mother's smile. The accusations. The uncomfortable moment with my father. Mom said my father won't be here, though; he's headed out of town for a convention tonight.

I'll add that to a list of things to be grateful for. At the very least I don't have to look into my father's eyes and wonder if he hits my mother.

With a clunk, the gas pump halts and the wind blows a colder air from the roaming hills and mountains off the highway. Goosebumps travel down my blouse and my gaze instantly moves to the back seat where my luggage rests and my coat remains draped over it. The cream sweater wrapped around my shoulders is made from crocheted yarn and the bitter air easily moves through the holes.

It's fine, I tell myself, ignoring this nagging feeling in my gut. Everything is fine for now.

It's only when I'm seated back in my car, with the *ding, ding, ding* from my keys resting in the ignition driving my irritation higher, that I read the texts again.

I turn on the car if for no other reason than to stop the incessant dinging. Both messages came within two minutes of each other, both as I veered off of the highway and onto these less traveled but somehow more worn paths. It must've been an hour after I left. Cody's first and then Marcus's.

To Cody I respond: *Just stopped for gas; I'll be there in two hours and text you then.*

A text, not a call. I realize there's a difference, but given that I'm going straight to my mother's and not the hotel, he can deal. Even if things hadn't changed between us, I still wouldn't call him when I got to my mother's. Calls are for emergencies and a text will do just fine. A churning in my gut refutes that statement, knowing I'd be pushing Cody away and not liking it in the least.

To Marcus, I fail to come up with a suitable response. He fed me information and all it did was prompt me to rattle off more questions. So I ask him, *If I had more questions, would you answer?*

Both men respond in the same way the initial messages arrived, one after the other, Cody's being first.

I'll talk to you soon. The response from Cody is exactly what I expected.

The exact same response from Marcus does nothing but give me chills: *I'll talk to you soon.*

With a shiver running down the length of my neck and trailing over my shoulders, I turn up the heat and head back onto the road.

Somewhere in the back of my mind, I know this is only a distraction and things are going to get worse. I'm only hiding.

I'm grateful to be hiding, though, and with every mile I

get closer to my mother's, I find myself watching the clock and wishing I were home.

For the first time, it's not my mother and sister who need me, I realize, it's me who needs them.

With hours to pass on my way up to my hometown and the radio playing, but my unwilling mind not listening, tiny memories come back to me. They seemed so insignificant, these little blips that didn't really matter when I was younger. But as I sit in the car, turning the heater on and off nearly as much as I shift in my seat, my critical eye taints the sweet memories.

One in particular never made sense.

Mom was sobbing when we got home from a trip that she didn't come on with us.

I can still hear her wretched cry of relief when we walked into the living room.

"Mom? What's wrong?" Cadence asked as I stood there in shock, a small doll hanging from my right hand. The floral backpack Cady wore had the gifts we brought back for Mommy. We were so excited to give them to her. All three of us, Daddy included.

Never in my little mind did I expect to come home to my mother crying on the floor of the living room.

"My babies," my mother cried out and swept Cady into a tight hug. I stayed back watching her sway; I'm sure my expression mirrored Cadence's shock. "Where were you?" She heaved in a

breath at the same time the question ran away from her.

"*We were good, so Daddy took us on a trip.*"

"*A trip?*"

"*Of course, Mommy.*" *My father's voice was far too upbeat at the sight of my mother crying and distraught. Didn't he see she was scared? He stood behind me in the kitchen, his large hands resting on my shoulders.* "*Silly Mommy,*" *he joked.* "*We're home,*" *he said and beamed with a bright smile. It was odd, everything about the moment. Maybe that's why I remember it so well.*

"*I got you taffy, Mommy,*" *I offered and my mother gripped me in the tightest hug, holding on to me and squeezing too tight. I didn't understand what was wrong with her. Our father said she was just being silly. Back then I felt awful, though, since she'd obviously wanted to come with us. That's what I thought.*

"Of course we came back. We'd never leave you." I think those were the words from my father. "Family doesn't ever leave."

At the time, I was so happy to see my mother smile, wiping under her tired eyes and clinging to me and my sister. We made her happy, although it didn't make sense that she was upset at all. We'd been good, our grades and our behavior both, so it was wonderful to be rewarded with a trip to the amusement park for the weekend. How could Mom not have known?

The realization never clicked. The pieces didn't add up and the questions stayed buried at the back of my memory where childish things that didn't matter went to die.

The crickets are already out and chirping noisily when I pull into the driveway. It's dark for only being seven but the fall brings early sunsets in this part of the country, especially in these Podunk towns in the mountains of northeastern New York.

The old fence in the backyard has been patched with newer pickets that stand out even in the dim illumination provided by the streetlights. They're a bright white among the dingy, worn paint of the others. The grass needs to be cut too. I imagine that's what my father would be doing this weekend if he weren't headed out for a conference. Vaguely I wonder what conference it is. If I was earlier in my career, I'd have already texted him and would have preferred to spend my weekend at the conference rather than the dinner and movie plans my sister concocted. That seems like a lifetime ago too.

Sitting back in my car I stare up at the two-story family home with dark red brick and cream shutters. So many memories are carved into the walls of this house. Good ones and bad ones both, but right now, all I can envision are the times I smiled along with my sister.

As our mother did our hair at the kitchen sink and all the

games of hide-and-seek that drove my father crazy. All the good times do little to settle the sadness that lingers in my chest. It's a weight that won't move and maybe that's because back then, there was so much hope. So much innocence.

All I can think is that little girl I used to be would be horrified by who I've become.

My eyes burn with the sting of exhaustion and something else. I grab my purse, leaving my luggage and coat where they are even though I'm certain it's bitter cold out there. It's always ten degrees colder up here than it is down in Pennsylvania.

There's an ominous feeling that greets me as I approach. After the large front door creaks open and shuts just as easily, there's only silence in the large old house. I can't remember a single time when it was this dark and quiet. "Hello?" I call out and expect my mother to shout down from upstairs. Maybe she's still getting ready.

The lights being out in the foyer don't help that strange feeling, so I flick them on as I call out for my mother, "Mom?"

A torn sob echoes from somewhere to the left, beyond the kitchen. I think it came from the living room.

"Mom?" I repeat, crying out as dread spreads through me and I pick up my pace. My keys rattle in my hands and my purse nearly slips as I get to the threshold.

My mother's there, on her knees on the floor and she doesn't stop crying as I approach. It's like she can't hear me.

"Mom, what's wrong?" The moment the question is

asked, my heart stops. There's blood. So much blood. But it's not touching her. I follow the pool and find it leads to my father. My purse drops along with my keys as my knees hit the stone floor hard.

My hands shake and I make my way toward him, inching myself along with my hands in the air as if to reach for him but they're held back.

There's so much blood and the smear of it in front of me, a smear from his leg being dragged through it is dried. With my right hand trembling, I place my palm on his back.

My mother's sobs still haven't stopped. My name is incoherent in her last cry as she rocks back and forth.

Breathe. He doesn't.

Tears flow freely down my face, stinging my eyes.

"Dad," I call out and then with the back of my hand, I press my fingers to his cheek. The second that skin touches skin, I pull back and push myself away.

His skin is cold as ice.

Thud, thud, my heart pounds and attempts to race, but it's like it's caught in free fall. It can't speed up or slow down, it simply is what it is.

"Mom ... what happened?" My question's strength is nonexistent. It's faint and full of the same fear that courses through my body.

Until I see the glint of metal next to my mother. A gun.

"You shot him?" I don't know how I'm even able to

question her. It's not real. Of course she didn't. She wouldn't kill him. She can't kill anyone. It's my mother.

Before I can apologize, my mom speaks.

"I had to, baby girl," my mother cries, tears streaming down her face, dragging the remains of mascara with it. With a sniff and a harsh wipe across her face, my mother's dark brown gaze stares down at my father's body. He lies on his stomach, blood soaking through his shirt and creating a halo of darkness around his face. It bleeds into his cheek, staining his skin.

There's no movement of his chest. No breathing, no blinking, no signs of life at all and vomit rises up my throat as my trembling fingers cover my mouth.

My entire body shakes, glancing between my dead father and my mother who just admitted she murdered him.

"I had to, Delilah ..." she whispers. "I had to."

"No," I say, denying it, shaking my head and crawling backward until my back hits the cabinets.

"You don't understand. I'm sorry. I'm so sorry."

"Mom, no," I whisper. The realization grips my shoulders the way I wish I could grip my mother and shake her. Shake her and demand she tell me the truth because this can't be real. She didn't do it.

With her bottom lip quivering and my mother's expression worn and full of pain, she looks me in the eye and tells me, "I'm sorry I didn't do it sooner."

Evidence convicts. Confessions can lead to convictions too, but as I drive exactly fifty-five miles per hour with my mother laying down in the back seat of my car, careful not to go over the speed limit, I refuse to let her confess to anything to anyone.

It doesn't make any sense. Not what my mother did and not what I did. I dragged her out of there as she pushed against me, fought me even. I pulled her away and I'll be damned if I'm going back there.

She's not going down for murder.

I won't let it happen.

"Lilah, baby," my mother pleads with me between the sobs.

"Shhh, Mom," I whisper and lick my bottom lip, tasting my own salty tears. "I just need time to think. I'll fix this. I promise," I tell her. I can't believe she did it. She didn't. My mind's at war with itself.

There's something missing, something wrong and I can't let anyone know until I know what really happened.

The convenience store sign is lit, but half of it is out when I pull into the Gas & Stop. I've been to this place countless times. It's stood here since I was a little girl. Around the corner there's a pay phone. I've waited for years for it to vanish like the rest of them have, but somehow it's remained.

I stop here every time I visit. And I've always thought the pay phone was only there for criminals and cheaters. As I park and release a breath I didn't know I was holding, telling my mother to just stay in the car for a moment, I realize this time I'm the criminal.

Fleeing the scene of a crime.

Aiding and abetting a criminal.

The charges whisper in the back of my mind as I dial one of the only numbers I know by heart.

The images flash through my mind as it rings and my hand slams against the booth as I brace myself.

She didn't do it. I lie to myself until my sister's voice is heard. "Hello?"

"Is anyone around you?" I ask her without telling her it's me. She'll know. She'll know it's me.

"What are you—"

"Answer me," I say and my tone is deathly low and I'm aware it must make my sister nervous.

"Of course," she answers and her breathing is heavier on the line now. "Yes," she says, strengthening her tone as she continues, "there is." There's someone around her. Someone who could watch her take this call and testify. Evidence. It's all about evidence right now.

"You're not talking to me, you're talking to a patient and everything is fine."

"What's going on?" Her voice is barely even but she makes

an effort to hide her fear. My own creeps up my arm like tiny spiders racing across my flesh. I can't believe I'm doing this. My expression crumples and pain runs through me as the memory of my mother on the floor flashes before my eyes. The blood. My father.

I struggle to speak, but heave in a breath, knowing I need to do this. "You're going to go to Mom's," I tell her and my voice gets tight. "And you're going to call the cops when you get there."

"Why ... why would I do that?" She corrects her tone, keeping it sounding light, but if someone's paying attention, this call is going to be suspicious.

"Remember," I say then swallow and brush under my eyes as I breathe out. "Someone could be watching you. You need to make it appear that this call is normal."

It takes a handful of breaths before my sister says, "Right, right. I know that. It's fine." I can just picture her standing there with her arms crossed and leaning casually against the wall. I hate that I have to tell her this way. *Forgive me. Lord, forgive me.*

"I cleaned up the evidence." My throat is tight and I find myself gripping the pay phone handset harder, both hands clinging to it as I stare at my car. I can't see her, but I know my mother lays in the back seat. When I parked, she was silently crying.

"Of what?" My sister's swallow is more audible than her

question.

"I'll explain it all to you after. But when you get home, we won't be there. You're going to call the cops and the last you heard from me were the texts we had earlier."

"Is it Mom?" my sister practically cries and I hush her, reminding her that she's talking to a patient.

"They're gone. They just left," my sister says in a breathy voice on the other end of the line, and it takes me a moment to realize she's referring to whoever was in the room with her. She heaves in a shuddering breath as if she's strangling on her words. "Did Mom kill herself?"

"What?" I ask and my heart races.

"I confronted her."

With a pounding in my pulse, I watch as a cop car rolls up to the red light outside the convenience store. I'm quick to turn my back so he can't see me. But that also means turning away from my car and my mother. Who's obviously in shock among every other reeling emotion that's taken her over.

"You confronted her about what?"

My sister begins to answer but I cut her off, not having the time. "Mom's okay." *Dad isn't...* The words are right there waiting to be spoken aloud but they don't come.

"And Dad?" she blurts out and I can't answer. "No, no ..." My sister's tone is wretched. "I should've kept my mouth shut," she says weakly. Even over the phone I can feel her breaking down.

"When you get home ... I need you to tell them I was supposed to be there with Mom and that we're missing. I'm going to try to clean it up."

"Dad?" my sister cries, and the back of my eyes prick. "They were fighting. I heard them."

"No!" I'm quick to shut her down and breathe out slowly. "No, you didn't. You didn't confront Mom about anything. Dad was supposed to be at a conference and we were having a girls' weekend. That is all you know," I say and I'm firm with her.

"You need to act normal but I wanted you to be prepared. I'm going to protect her. I promise," I tell my sister although the pieces of how exactly I'm going to do just that still haven't come together in my mind. The sound of traffic moving along allows me to peek over my shoulder, finding the cop car gone and my own sitting there, waiting for me. "I'm going to protect her from this."

"She killed him, didn't she?" My sister guesses the truth and all I can tell her is that I love her and to take care of what I asked her to do.

It's a sickening feeling as I get back to my car. Like the world is crumbling around me and there's nothing I can do to hold it up.

Chapter 8

Delilah

"You're my baby girl," my father tells me in that singsong way that lets me know he's in a good mood. "No one's ever going to hurt you."

"I'll protect you too, Daddy," I'm happy to tell him back. "That's what I'm going to do. I'm going to protect people."

"Oh yeah?"

"I'm going to grow up and be just like you."

"You think so?" he asks me and I nod my head in response to his raised brow.

"That's what we decided last night."

"We?" he asks. As we walk down Main Street to the post office, I hold his hand and he swings it to and fro. When we get to the block before the post office, I skip over all the dark lines of *the cracked pavement.*

"*Cady is going to be like Mom and I'm going to be like you.*"

Don't step on a crack or you'll break your mother's back. The children's rhyme plays in my head.

"*All right then. That sounds like your mother and I are doing a good job then, huh?" Daddy's smile is bright and the sky behind him the prettiest shades of blue. There's not a cloud in sight. "I'd say so," I answer him. My father. My hero.*

I must've been around five in my earliest memories of my father. His handsome face barely resembles the man on the floor of my parents' living room, the man with the face lined with worry and aged from the passage of time.

With sweaty palms, I have to grip the wheel tighter before wiping off the moisture on my pants and getting a grip.

He's dead. My father's dead. The prickly harshness in the back of my throat is a precursor to crying but I hold it back. Not yet. I can't lose both my parents. I can't lose them both.

"Where are we going?" My mother's voice wavers as she rises up, her reddened eyes peering into mine in the rearview mirror. The hand over her mouth quivers slightly. Maybe the reality is sinking in.

"Somewhere for us to hide for a moment, get you cleaned up—"

"You need to turn back." She's firmer than when she voiced her initial question, but altogether her tone lacks strength. I imagine doing what she did took it all away from her.

"No, Mom." I swallow thickly and speak to her as if what I'm saying is fact; there's not an ounce of negotiation in my tone. "We're twenty minutes from the hotel."

I've got cash in my purse, cash that's meant for my sister to pay her back for the last salon visit.

"Turn back now." Her hardened voice used to scare me when I was a child. Even into my teen years. My mother hardly ever yelled. That's what our father was there for. All the discipline. Hearing it now, though ... she just sounds desperate.

The *tick, tick, tick* of the turn signal follows us down Asher Lane. I recognize the street and know the hotel is only one block down. It's in a quiet area, small and close to the off-ramp to the highway. It's an old building and used to be some kind of chain. Everything about it screams dated but I guess the owner sold the place rather than updating it.

"Gunshot residue doesn't lie and you need somewhere to wash it all off, plus a change of clothes."

"I shouldn't have done this," she says and my mother's statement is a plea. As if she wishes she could go back. I've heard that cadence so many times. "Just take me back."

"I'm not taking you back until I make sure you're all right."

"Did you see what I did?" she says and her voice cracks. With a shuddering breath she croaks out, "You shouldn't have to deal with me. I'm so sorry. I'm so sorry, my baby girl."

"No talking now. Please, just wait." It's always a struggle

when a child watches their parent break down. But right now? It feels like that bullet went straight through my heart.

"Let me get you inside."

"Don't help me. I don't deserve it." She begs me as I pull into the parking lot.

"I don't know, but ..." I trail off as I struggle to justify anything I've done.

"You don't know what he did." Pain lingers in each of her words. "I couldn't ... I didn't know it all. I just thought ... Oh God ..." My mother's sobs wrack through her and she rocks back and forth. A shivering chill flows over me as I slam the car into park.

Something's been broken for a very long time. More broken than the cracks I skipped over as my father held my hand down Main Street.

How did I ignore it? Waves of heat and anxiety crash within me. Suddenly I need the cold air outside just to breathe.

The lot is mostly vacant. Which is expected. It's not like this town gets a lot of tourism.

There are a few cars, all of which are much older models than my own.

I turn back to look at my mother, wanting to calm her down or at least make sure she knows to stay here for just a moment. The seat groans loud and heavy as my mother sways with a hand over her heart, her face tilted up to the roof of the car. Like she's praying.

"I want you to tell me everything."

"Don't risk—"

I smack the passenger seat to get her attention. Her eyes whip up at me.

"I've already abandoned the scene of a crime. I'm going in that office right there, getting a room and then I need you to tell me everything." I spoke it all too quickly. But I got it out at least. Licking my cracked bottom lip, I wait for her to say something, anything.

The nod of my mother's head is subtle, but she agrees. "I'll stay here."

I'm firmer this time, like I am with the defendants. "I'm going to need you to tell me everything."

My mother hesitates but again, she gives me that small nod of agreement. Not wasting another second, I get out of the car and the cold air is nothing but brutal and refreshing at once.

Sniffing and wiping under my eyes, I brace myself to face the first person I have to encounter, a potential witness.

The check-in area isn't any larger than six by six feet. A counter spans the length of the room and behind it there's a plain white door that I imagine leads to a back hall or closet.

As I place my hand on the sign-in sheet, wanting to tap it instead of the bell, attempting to get the attention of the man laying back in the chair, his feet up on the counter and a hat over his face, I see under my sleeve of the cream sweater.

There's just a spot of blood on it.

My father's blood. My own runs cold as I pull my arm back just in time for the old man to lift the hat from his head.

"Didn't hear you come in." He speaks while rubbing his eyes with just one hand and then pinching the bridge of his nose. "Allergies always get me this time of year. Excuse me," he says and then blinks away whatever sleep he was attempting to get.

"A room for tonight. Maybe the weekend?" I ask and even to my own ears I sound out of breath.

My tone gets the man's attention. He glances away from me to look past me.

"Just you?" he asks and I nod. It's a lie, but better that than the truth. Why the hell would I get a motel room for me and my mother when she lives in town?

"How much?" I ask, already prying out my wallet and counting the bills.

I've stayed here plenty of times. It's only sixty-five dollars for the night. He tells me one hundred and I hand it over in a single bill. He eyes it for a second too long before taking it.

It's only then I can breathe. "Thank you."

"You all right?" he asks, his lips in a thin line.

I let out a sigh and close my eyes before telling him, "It's been one hell of a drive and it's way too cold for September."

The clerk huffs a laugh while the register clangs open. "It's only going to get colder this weekend."

With everything that happened, I didn't realize my mother was wearing a dress. The top part is a solid navy blue, which complements the bottom portion that's a dark blue paisley. I also didn't realize she wasn't wearing shoes. She ran out in her slippers and I didn't pay attention to that either.

I'm sure there's plenty I missed. I got the part where she shot my father and laid there for hours sobbing next to him, though. *Hours.* She sat there next to him for hours. The prosecutor in me would have a field day with that fact alone.

Unbuttoning the top button of her dress, I wonder if she planned on a girls' night out to a nice restaurant downtown when she put it on. I bet she thought today was going to be a good day. It was one worth dressing up for.

She didn't get to her hair or makeup, though. Or else it all came undone when the altercation happened. I can't ask the first question that's begging to be brought to life. *Did he hit you, Mom? Did he threaten you?* I don't want to bring it up, just as much as she doesn't want to talk about it.

The navy cotton fabric slips down her arms easily as I help her out of it. She hasn't said a word, but her eyes are drenched in worry and tragedy and unspoken questions.

I don't think I've ever seen my mother scared. Not like this.

"There you go," I barely get out as the fabric falls to the

floor and I wonder if my father saw her like this. Is that wretched look what she wore when she pulled the trigger?

The steam in the shower builds, fogging the top of the mirror's edge and the warmth is positively suffocating. I busy myself rubbing my sore shoulder and barely watch her from my periphery in the foggy mirror as she slips down the rest of her dress and climbs into the tub.

The clothes will have gunshot residue on them too.

The hot water splashes and with it is the sound of my luggage unzipping as I pull out the toiletries I packed.

The goal is simple enough: get rid of the residue, calm my mother down, and come up with a plausible defense.

A nagging voice in the back of my mind whispers to ask her why. Swallowing thickly, I ignore it. But when I close my eyes, every little moment I ignored before flashes before me.

I pray this hot water can cleanse away these sins.

"You ran to find the killer." I speak as I set a bottle on the edge of the tub. With the curtain pulled back, I can't see her and she can't see me.

"You were distraught at your husband's death and how it happened so fast, there was nothing you could do."

My body sways, my breath stolen for a moment as I envision a different reality. "But you saw the man." With a heavy exhale I place a second bottle next to the first and tell her to wash her hair. My mother hasn't moved, hasn't spoken.

"I went into the foyer but no one was there and then I

saw you running out the back. I saw something or someone else first but I didn't get a good look, but I saw you and ran out, wondering what the hell you were doing. I chased after you and when I finally got to you, you were trying to hurt yourself, sobbing uncontrollably."

"Trying to hurt myself?"

"It lays a claim that you weren't in your right mind."

"Though in your version," she starts and my mother's words are spoken both slowly and lowly, "I was after the real killer?" I glance up at her as tears streak down her face.

"You were, you were running after him after you found Daddy dead, but he got away and you couldn't take it."

"As if they'd believe I could run faster than you." My mom offers her doubt. "I could just tell them the truth."

Ignoring her comments, I continue. "You were too scared to go back inside. I thought you were having an episode. I was going to take you to the hospital, not having seen anything inside, until you begged me not to. You just wanted to leave, to get away so I did that. I made that happen, not understanding what had happened."

"That's what you've got, baby girl?" My mother's question is nothing but melancholy.

"You fell asleep, then in the morning you told me everything."

"I don't want you to lie for me," my mother says and it's then I see she still hasn't touched the shampoo.

When I don't respond and instead grab the shampoo and force it into her hands, she speaks. "I thought he cheated on me," my mother says, her voice tight with the confession. "I swear, back then I thought he was cheating and I didn't know."

"Didn't know what, Mom?" I'm too scared to ask and when I do, she looks down at me, the steam flowing around her.

With a wobbly smile that doesn't reach her eyes, she shakes her head and says, "Nothing, baby."

"Mom, what happened?" I ask and tears stream from my eyes just as they do from hers.

"He did it for the last time. I had to."

"He hit you?" I say my guess in a whisper and my mother's weak smile broadens with sympathy. "Yeah, baby, he hit me."

"I'm sorry." I barely get out the words, bracing myself against the cheap cabinet of the sink.

"When you and your sister were little," my mother interjects, "you two were as thick as thieves and I remember praying you'd stay close like I wish me and my sisters were."

I can't even think of Cadence right now and what she's about to walk in on. My heart breaks today for so many reasons; I don't know how it still beats.

"You remember that time you ate all the candy from the canister? I found it empty and called you two in."

"You knew it was me the whole time?" I ask her, knowing just how this story plays out.

My mother nods her head. "Cadence was so quick to take

the fall for you. And that time she stained the back seat of your auntie's Buick, you took the blame for that one."

The past events play out before me. We were just two sisters getting into normal trouble.

"You two were always looking out for each other."

"Mom, what's this have to do with Dad?" I ask and she only shakes her head, finally opening the bottle of shampoo. "Nothing, baby girl. I just want you to know I love you. I love you both so much and you can't stop loving each other. Even if you stop loving me."

Using a wad of toilet paper, I stop the tears from flowing but stay in the bathroom, the shower curtain closed so I can't see behind it.

It's quiet a long time, other than bottles opening and silent tears being swept away.

"You're throwing your career away doing this," my mother warns and a piece of me is all too aware of that possibility.

"You better get good at lying then. And holding on to that story, Mom. Because I don't want to lose my job, but I'll be damned if I lose you."

With a harsh swallow I repeat what I just came up with as if it just happened. "I came home and no one was there but someone caught my eye as they ran out to the backyard. And then I saw you running into the woods. I was going to take you to the hospital because you wouldn't stop crying and tried to hurt yourself." I add in that last detail. "And I almost took you in, but you begged me not to."

Rising to my feet, my body aches and my bones crack. Carefully, I pull back the shower curtain and pour out more than enough conditioning treatment as my mother's head hangs in shame, and I lather it. I make sure to get it all, refusing to let any residue stay behind.

"I didn't do it, I didn't bring you in, because of what happened last month," I whisper and my mother's composure cracks. "They're going to know about it, Mom, and it's motive so it's best we bring it up and control the narrative."

She's silent as I work the conditioner through her hair and then comb it through. "It needs to sit," I tell my mother and she nods. The water's still hot and the steam smothers me.

"Ask for a lawyer, speak as little as possible. I have the story and I'll make sure it'll stick. You just have to be quiet as much as you can and stick with the story I gave you."

It's quiet for the rest of the time, the hot water splashing onto my arms and chest when I rinse out her hair. It soaks into my sleeve where the blood resided and I watch the pink droplets fall into the tub. I'll throw away the clothes. All of them and buy new ones for my mother in the morning.

Over and over in my head, I rehearse our story and hope it's our way out of this.

My mother's only silent or crying, nothing more than that until she tries to confide in me, "I wish …"

My motions stop, the lather on my hands a stark pure

white and smelling sweetly of lavender.

This time when I ignore her, when I don't press for more, I know why I'm doing it. I'm not strong enough to handle any more than this tonight. "There won't be a damn shred of evidence to tie you to this when you go in for questioning. Don't give them any. Don't give them a damn thing."

"What'd you do with the gun?"

"It's wiped down, and it's Dad's, isn't it?" I know it is. It doesn't make sense to hide it when there are no fingerprints and they'll know the gun that killed him matches the one he has registered.

"You will not go to prison for this. I swear by it." Holding back the emotions I'm feeling, and relying on the ruthless lawyer inside of me, I step away and tell her to comb the leave-in conditioner through, as if she doesn't know.

"I'll leave these sweats for you." My mother's a bit larger than I am, but they'll fit. My pajamas are always baggy and loose. She'll be fine tonight in them.

Leaving them on the sink, I leave the bathroom, worn and damaged in a way that hits me the moment the cool air batters my skin. With the click of the door behind me, I lean my head back as shuddering breaths leave me.

My father's dead. My mother's a murderer.

And my mind can't wrap itself around those facts. Fresh tears threaten as my phone sounds out. Sniffling, I pull myself together.

Cody's called. Multiple times.

My sister's called but she didn't leave a voicemail.

No one else. So I don't think she's gotten home yet. She hasn't made the discovery or called the cops. In the mindset of supporting my story, I should turn off my phone. And so that's what I do right now. I hold down the button on the side until the screen turns black, shutting out the world and hiding. Just for one night.

And what about tomorrow? It's Cody's voice that questions me. The guilt of it squeezes like a vise around my chest.

I can't tell him anything. Not any part of the truth. I can lie to the police all day, I can turn an interrogation into a children's story. But Cody? He'll see through it all, and I can't confess to him.

The one person I want to talk to is the one who's gotten away with murder—the one I need to make sure I don't lose my mom too.

I help my mother brush her hair when she's finally out of the bathroom and lying down on the bed. I brush her hair like she used to do for me.

When her chest falls and rises steadily, and I know she's sleeping, I stand on weak legs. I clean it all up, tossing the clothes at the bottom of the tub, and rinsing them down.

I let them soak before tossing them out. There's no reason to keep them, but if somehow they're found, they'll at least be clean of residue.

When I get back into the room, well after midnight with new clothes from the 24/7 Walmart two towns over, there's a faint knock on the wall.

Knock, knock, knock knock knock … knock, knock.

Like a child. Like I used to do with my sister in the house and my father when he went up to the old barn.

As I get closer to it, the sequence comes again.

Knock, knock, knock knock knock …

I hesitantly reach out my hand and respond: *knock, knock.*

Chapter 9

Marcus

I woke up to the soft cries of the boy who was huddled in the corner opposite of mine in the cell.

I know what that means and I swallow the jagged rock lodged in my throat that seems to block my voice.

It took a long time for either of us to speak. We've been here for … at least a week together, but he was here longer. I don't know how long and I don't want to ask. I don't want to remind him of the first time.

I can trace every outline of my ribs. It tickles slightly when I do it and yesterday I did it so much the skin on my right side feels raw and still tingles when anything brushes against it. Sleep takes up most of the day and night. It's easier to sleep now than it was before. The first few days I was terrified they'd come if I closed my eyes, but now I know they barely come at all. Unless we do something against the rules, they stay upstairs and forget about us. That's what I pray for, for them to forget about us, even if that means we don't eat for days.

The soft sound of his throat clearing comes with a hollow look. There's a darkness around his eyes; I'm certain mine must mirror his.

"Do you think they're gone?" he whispers and I nod although I don't make the nod too obvious. They have cameras to keep an eye on us and they don't like us talking. They let the dogs in if we talk. I don't want to see the dogs. He knows that. I'm certain he does.

It's so quiet that I can hear when his head thuds against the wall. Looking in his direction, his eyes are closed and he looks as tired as I feel. But more than that, he's terrified.

"How did you get here?" I ask just to say something to distract him from his own mind, but I hate the unspoken follow-up question that begs to be asked.

"I was walking home from school," he says and as he answers his pointer finger draws on the cement. From the other side of the cell, I can't see what he's tracing.

"Where do you go to school?"

"I don't know the name but my teacher is Miss Harrow. She teaches the kindergarteners."

He's younger than me. I almost ask him how old he is

and what his name is, but the door to the upstairs suddenly opens. My first thought is that they're sending down the dogs but it's not. It's worse. Much worse.

My shoulders slam against the brick wall as I hear a loud clang of a gate followed by a grunt. They're back. Terrified eyes pierce into mine and with a quick and rushed movement, I gesture for the boy to come over to my side of the cell. His bare feet leave a sound I wish was the only sound I could hear, a pattering of small feet on the damp ground.

But the heavy boots outweigh the pitter-patter and even more so a muffled cry. A small voice that begs for help. The boy trembles next to me, smaller, weighing less and wearing less too. He's cold, so cold but the shaking is from the same fear that works its way through my bones. My right arm wraps around his small body and I try to stay strong for him, forcing my eyes to stay open as we huddle in the corner farthest away from the iron gate. I watch because he doesn't, he closes his eyes tight. One of us has to watch. This time it's me.

"Shhh." I hush him as his whimpers get louder. They're almost here. The two men I know in my nightmares. There's oil on their hands. I think it's oil; it's all I can smell when they come. They smell like the garage used to when my father's car broke down.

The one on the right, the tall one and older one heaves the cell gate opposite ours open. The shorter one who's heavier tosses the bag into the cell and a vicious crack sounds out followed by a shriek of pain.

Hot tears leak down my face, but I don't look away. I have to make sure they stay over there, in that cell and not ours. And they do. The gate closes, locking with a click that will haunt me forever, and I watch because someone has to and the boy can't.

The screams don't stop for hours.

Chapter 10

Delilah

My *mother killed my father.* The statement is fit for a tragedy, maybe one of Shakespeare's plays. I hated English Lit in college. I only took the class because I had to. All the while I remember tapping my pencil against the textbook as I did the assigned readings, thinking how unrealistic it was. How outdated and far too dramatic the stories were as they unfolded.

As my mother lies on the edge of the queen bed, I can't help but to be brought back to that moment, and suddenly I feel foolish. *How did this happen?*

With trembling hands, I close my eyes and pretend like it's only a story. I don't know if it's the adrenaline that kept me from thinking about the reality ... but my mother killed my father.

And I'm helping her get away with it.

Knock, knock, knock knock knock ... The pattern of five faint knocks on the door to the hotel room draws my eye to the dull white door. A shadow is vaguely seen creeping from under the locked door.

My heart slams against my rib cage as a slip of paper slides under the crack.

Even from where I sit, huddled with my knees pulled into my chest and my eyes burning from lack of sleep and the prick of former tears, I can see the dark scribbles of handwriting.

The second the paper lands on the worn, thin carpet, the shadow disappears and it's quiet again with the exception of heavy footsteps outside, followed by the creak of the next room's door opening. I sit there, very much aware that it has to be Marcus who's next door. It must be him. And more importantly ... he must know what happened or that something has happened. How else would he have found me?

How much does he know? The question lingers as my body stays frozen.

Knock, knock. The last two taps of the game I remember from my childhood come through the wall only feet from me.

A shudder runs through me and I can only look back at my mother, still sleeping. Unaware of the fear that keeps me crippled in this chair.

A second passes and then another before the realization

sinks in that I'd rather go to him than have him come here. I don't know how I'm able to move my horrified limbs, but I do, bending down to read the slip of paper with the simple command on it.

Come over.

With a deep breath in I slip on my flats, once again staring at my mother's sleeping form. Even in her rest, there's a crease etched in the center of her forehead and her brow is pinched. Even in her sleep, she's plagued by what's happened. There's no escape from it.

As I creep out of the room, all I can think is that she really did it. This is happening and I'm caught in the middle of it all.

Hesitation overwhelms me as I stand on the outdoor walkway in front of the room next door. The small peephole is a black pupil that stares back at me as the chill of the fall night air wraps itself around my shoulders.

With the back of my hand, I barely form a fist and rap: *Knock, knock. Knock knock knock* ... I don't have to finish. On the last knock, and with an eerie creak, the door opens. Not enough for me to go through, but enough to see the bathroom light is on inside. No other light, just the one and it barely bathes the room in the dim yellow glow.

"Hello?" I call out, my voice raspy and not at all sounding like myself. Clearing my throat, I gently push the door open wider. My heart races until I hear his voice.

"Come in. I've been waiting."

Thump, thump, it all slows when I hear how calm and expectant he is. The deep baritone comes from the far left of the room. His room's the same as mine, only mirrored. So his bed touches the wall where mine is placed. It's only inches from where my mother sleeps.

That knowledge sends goosebumps down my back.

"Didn't mean to keep you," I tell him although I'm unsure where the response comes from. All of it is surreal and I find myself praying to just wake up.

"You were busy with your mother, that's understandable."

Thump, thump. The tips of my fingers go numb as I make my way to the chair seated in front of a simple desk. The other would be more comfortable, but it's closer to him.

At the thought, my gaze lifts and I see more of him than I did before. For a moment, only a split second, I think he's Cody, not Marcus.

With his dirty blond hair, just a bit too long to be Cody Walsh, and the width of his shoulders, he looks so much like him.

My head spins and I lean forward in the chair, unable to hide my reaction. Maybe I just wish Cody were here. I wish it were him sitting there.

"I look like him, don't I?" he asks and there's a pain present in his tone. Undoubtedly so.

"You do," I say and a shudder runs through me at the admission.

"They used to say, never to us but to each other, the boy and I could be brothers."

My heart pangs in my chest and I swallow thickly as I look up at him. "The boy?" I ask but Marcus only shakes his head.

"I'm sorry. I shouldn't have brought it up. You must have so much on your mind."

The words jumble at the back of my throat and my gaze shifts to the light from his bathroom. The door is open and I can clearly see the shower curtain pulled back. I bathed her to get rid of evidence. I'm an accomplice to murder.

My father's murder.

My head hangs lower and I have to part my lips to take in a shaky breath.

"You don't want to talk about it?" Marcus asks.

My hands tremble as I pull my knees up and sit so damn uncomfortably on the small chair. My back leans against the wooden slats and my shoulders rest on the barely padded back of it.

"Do you know what happened?" I whisper, although I already know the answer.

"I do," Marcus says. He stretches his legs out on the bed, still sitting up against the headrest. He's taller and leaner than Cody. I take it all in. Some awful, devious voice whispers in the back of my mind that I could leverage what's known about Marcus and his crimes. I could save my mother that way.

And myself.

With a quick shake of my head and a gut-churning sickness, I cover my eyes and drown that thought.

If I tried that, I'd be dead. Although as it stands, I may be dead already. The rabbit hole Alice fell down and the ridiculous plays they made us read in school ... none of it was as fucked up and unreal as this.

"Have you come up with a plan?" Marcus asks and I tell him.

I spit out the story I told my mother three times tonight and I'll tell her again tomorrow.

Marcus's response is merely a murmured *hmm*. Prolonged and drawn out, lacking in either approval or disapproval.

"Why are you here?" The venom in my tone is shocking and judging by the tilt of Marcus's head, giving more light to the left side of his face although it's still dark from where he lies, it shocks him as well. I hold on to the strength. I ask, "Am I collateral? Is this blackmail?"

The dim light gives a sheen to his teeth as he smirks with a huff. Readjusting against the headboard, the bed groans before he answers, "To see if you were all right."

The sick feeling from earlier drops into the pit of my stomach as my gaze lowers to the foot of the bed. Then I dare to look back up at him as he readjusts once more.

"And to give you an out. I could help with your mother." The world stops for a moment, my lungs stilling completely as I watch him reach to the nightstand to hold up a pad of paper. "I left a note behind. Thought you should know." The thud of the pad hitting the end table is followed by Marcus's comment. "I'm not sure your sister is expecting it, but given how bad of a liar she is, it'll only help your mother."

"You didn't implicate my sister—" My words are rushed as I scoot closer to the edge of the chair, desperation overwhelming me.

Marcus's tsk cuts me off. "I'm here to help, little mouse. Be careful, be quiet … and what I've set into motion will be good enough."

"What does it say?" I ask. When he doesn't immediately answer, I add to clarify, "The note. What did you leave?"

"It's of no concern to you. It would lead to more questions because you're missing so much of the story."

"Tell me then," I plead with him, my throat going dry.

"More questions for questions?" Marcus asks and the sibilant sound of each S lingers like the hiss of a snake. Goosebumps rake down my body, the memories of the other night more than eager to replace the fear that lays over every inch of me.

"It seems like you have more answers than I do." The thudding in my chest beats faster, but this time for a different reason. The small room is suddenly suffocating and there's not enough room to separate us. It's one sided and so very obvious.

Ignoring my comment completely, Marcus says, "Cody's a bit hung up but he had a feeling. He's perceptive like that."

My eyes close as I sit back, letting the low blow make

me feel even lower. I have no words although I wish I could respond. I love him. I love the man and I know I do. But he's a liar and I don't trust him.

"He blames himself, if that helps. And he'll fight for you." Lifting my eyes to Marcus's pale blue gaze, I keep my questions to myself.

"Maybe a smoke would help?" he says. He's toying with me. That's what this is to him, a cat and mouse game. That must be where he gets that nickname for me from. Anger would normally be my response. It should be. But it's entirely absent from my reaction to the slight. The wash of sadness is just as unexpected and only adds salt to the wound.

I watch as Marcus opens the drawer to the nightstand and lights a blunt.

With a puff of smoke, he offers it to me, but I shake my head. "I don't smoke."

He takes his time inhaling deeply before gesturing to the small fridge. "Wine it is then," he tells me. I'm frozen in the small chair, watching this powerful man let out a cloud of smoke from between his teeth, the white and black playing among the shadows.

"Don't be shy. I thought you'd need something more ... but maybe not."

"Something more?" I ask and force myself out of the chair, forcing myself to play his game if for no other reason than the fact that I can't do anything else. And my mother needs him.

Fuck, I need him.

The fridge is small and the single bottle of white wine has been placed inside at an angle so that it fits neatly. "Thank you for chilling it ..." I tell him and then spot a small plastic black bag on top of the dresser to the left. I recognize it as generic to liquor stores and inside of it I find a corkscrew and two plastic cups.

My fingers rest on both cups, my rational and logical side failing me. Silently, I hold up the cups, offering him one, but he shakes his head. The silence turns to a faint ringing in my ears that gets louder and louder. The images of today crash through me like a tidal wave as I open the bottle and pour the wine.

Chapter 11

Marcus

One cup of wine and her red eyes glisten. It's a good distraction, asking her about Cody. She's more defensive than anything when it comes to him … when it comes to us.

Two cups and her stiff shoulders loosen while her answers start to come easier. Her reluctance falls just as she does, slowly falling to pieces as I feed her clues bit by bit.

He did something a long time ago and her mother put the pieces together. I'm not sure Delilah is following the little breadcrumbs I'm giving her. She'll blink one day and see it all. Tonight I think she's simply looking for a distraction.

Her mother wouldn't have been able to, if he hadn't started up again. If I hadn't helped her along. Not that I added that last little piece out loud for Delilah. She doesn't need to know. All she has to fully accept is that he had done something bad and that her mother didn't mean it. Just like the sweet alcohol, it offers her the smallest sips of peace.

"Don't cry," I say, consoling her as she sniffs again, closing her eyes and pretending like she isn't on the verge of breaking down. I've seen so many men and women respond to death. It's almost always the same. Delilah's different. I attribute that to her cases and how hard it tried to make her. Or rather, how hard she tried to make herself so she could continue. So she could make it all make sense.

We all have our limits, though.

"Ask me something else ... something about us." Her dark chestnut gaze meets mine. Every time she looks at me, she centers. More than likely refusing to let go of this opportunity where she can use me. She could have so many questions answered, resolve so many of those cases that keep her up at night. And the riddles between myself and Cody would be revealed if only she asked the right questions. If only she could pull herself together. If only she could trust me enough.

We have time, little mouse. She'll get there.

She doesn't ask me any of that, though, as she grabs the bottle, eager to pour the last bits. "You watched me?" she asks with her back to me. The thin pajama pants hang loose on her hips and the burgundy tank top hugs her tempting curves.

"Yes."

"You stalked me?" she says and the empty bottle lands

with a clink on the dresser. She sips her drink with her back to me.

"Yes."

"For years?"

I hesitate only a moment before saying, "Yes."

Finally, she soothes my anxiousness, turning around to face me and she leans against the dresser. She's gorgeous when she's full of accusations.

"Why?"

I can't help but smile at her. Years ... she knows. But *how many years?* is the question she's still lacking.

I answer her the only way I know how. "If only I could tell you." Why do any of us torture ourselves with the things we can't have?

"Tell me something." For the first time, she gives me a demand and it makes me harder for her than I've ever been.

"And you'll tell me something in return?" There's only a slight movement from me in response to my eagerness. The tips of my fingers slip against the bedsheets. As if that would be enough to ground me ... as if it would hold me back.

"Of course," she says, whispering her answer and then biting down on her bottom lip. My cock stirs at the motion. I've never been a giving soul. There's always a selfish reason.

"You saw them for what they were." I speak without thinking.

"What do you mean?" Curiosity knits her brow.

"Just like the case last month ... Ross Brass." At the mention of his name, Delilah stops the cup midway to her lips. A coldness flickers in her gaze.

"It's not all black and white. It's covered in as much gray as it is blood. But once you see them for what they are, you don't let go."

Perhaps she'd rather I talk about anything other than herself because her mind wanders. I'm certain she thinks of her mother again. Or her father. It's given away by the drop of her gaze and the slower rate of her breathing.

"Do you want to know what I think?" I ask her and my throat is suddenly tight.

Confusion is apparent in her dark brown eyes and I'm certain she almost asks, *about what?*, but instead she only nods a yes. Maybe two cups have already been two too many.

"I think it will be all right but it will take a few days and you'll be just as anxious every day. Each day more anxious than the last until they have another name. Someone else to blame for your father's death. I think that's what you'll need to move past the worry."

"It will be all right?" Skepticism laces her question. It's almost sarcastic.

"With the note I left, no one will want to pin it on your mother. They'll have someone else in mind."

"Who?" she asks in a single breath.

"Someone who deserves to die."

"You're an angel of death," she says as if it's fact and I can only laugh. "That's what they tell me."

My amusement is a short but deep rumble in my chest. Her hips sway slightly and I pat the bed next to me, getting her attention.

I wait for her as she walks slowly to the very end of the bed and sits. I'm well aware she can see me, really see me if she looked up. Her eyes would have adjusted to the dark by now. My pulse races and just as she's about to, just as her thick lashes raise, I tell her to go turn off the light first.

"Turn it off and come back." She hums and doesn't hesitate to rise from the bed, making a soft groan.

She can't see me yet. Not yet, not just yet. Panic flows through my veins as the floor creaks with her gentle movements and she turns off the sole light that was on in the bathroom.

"So you are an angel of death?" she asks as the light disappears with a soft click.

"I don't decide, though? Do I?" I say to her, bringing her attention back to the conversation as she comes back to me like the good girl she is.

"They're going to die, regardless. I simply pull strings so it flows easier. So they kill each other and the victims, the ones who would fall pray to them otherwise, are reduced. That's not so wrong, is it?"

Delilah's quiet, so silent that I hear the moment the plastic cup, nearly empty now, hits her bottom lip.

"Like your cases. The ones they tampered with and never solved. They made that decision and it led to ... whatever it is it leads to ..." I debate confessing, but I can't help myself.

I can practically feel the way her pulse ramps up when I tell her, "I did you a favor, I closed them."

"This isn't the game we play," Delilah says, not asking about the cases I know she seeks answers to for refuge. I should have known better. She doesn't care about those cases right now. Not in the least. There's only one murder on her mind. "Did she do it because he hit her? Can you tell me that?" Back to her mother ...

No. The answer is there on the tip of my tongue, but I can't bring myself to say it. Then I would have to tell her. And that's a depressing conversation for another day.

"If your mother had pressed charges, what do you think would have happened?"

"He wouldn't have been found guilty. He would have kept it quiet and they would have split." Tears muffle her words.

"Not to him ... to her. What would have happened to her?" I have to remind the disappointment in me that she's too close to it and too uncertain of so many things. Too conflicted like Cody can be. It's not her fault that she didn't think of the other piece. No one ever thinks of the other one. The victim and what's left behind. As if a punishment makes those wrongs all right.

Her inhale is quicker, louder, but she remains silent.

"I don't want to talk about it." Finally. We agree on something tonight. The pieces are in motion, and there's nothing left to do but allow the dominoes to fall.

Before I can relish in leaving this conversation alone for the night, Delilah stands, readying herself to leave perhaps. But first she tosses the empty cup into the small bin by the desk. "Thank you for ... covering for my mother."

"And for you," I remind her, suddenly feeling hotter than I'd like.

My fingers itch, eager to keep her here. Again, they skip across the sheet, this time with more desperation.

"I don't like seeing you like this," I say, barely getting out the words. Even though it's nearly pitch black and the sounds from beyond the door fill the silence with both the chirps of crickets and the rushing of cars passing along the road, all I can hear is my heart beating as she crosses her arms against her chest.

At the sight of her breasts rising, my cock stiffens.

"I owe you," she tells me, but she already owes me more than she could imagine.

"You do," I say, agreeing with her admission and my tone gives her pause.

The day she came into that barn is the day he stopped. Every monster has a boundary. Look at what good came from such an awful man. At first, my fascination was simply due to watching out for her. She was his keeper in a way and I had so much to learn from him.

But it grew to be more. I don't know how or why.

I had a chance to kill him years ago, and didn't. So many chances and at some point I had to admit, I allowed him to live because of her.

I settled on a threat instead. The fool should have never set out to pick up his old habit.

Rather than counting up her debt, I happily contribute to it and say, "I have something to help you sleep if you need it."

I can hear her swallow from all the way over here.

"It's called sweets."

"My father told me not to take candy from strangers—" she starts to say but then stops herself midword. With an instant pang of sadness and regret evident on her beautiful face.

With her head falling back, her bottom lip drops as her mouth opens and sorrow overwhelms her inhale. She's trying to stifle her cries.

"Come here," I say. It's a demand and I'm not sure how she'll take it, so I soften my next words as I add, "Let me make you feel better."

Chapter 12

Delilah

It's not the wine. I can't tell you the number of defendants I've seen in the courtroom who blamed their actions on alcohol. It's never the buzz of a night out that's to blame for what they've done. Never.

We do the things we want to do. It's that simple.

If it wasn't already planted in the back of our minds, the seeds of the action wouldn't exist.

So it's not the wine. As much as I'd like to believe it is. The sweet taste is still on my lips as I stare across the dark room at a man who terrifies yet excites me.

I could claim my actions before were due to curiosity. I could claim that I wanted information, not unlike an undercover detective. In fact, that excuse had lingered on the tip of my tongue ever since those first unforgivable thoughts entered my vivid imagination.

Marcus's large hand smooths the comforter beside him. My body is heavy and weak; every piece of me is practically lead, weighed down in this moment.

Hot, molten lead, to be more specific. Unable to keep its form and desperate for somewhere to go.

There's not a single soul I could have confided in. Not one ... not even Cody.

No one but the man who beckons me to come lie with him. And if I'm honest with myself, it's something I've wanted since he first whispered my name.

Swallowing thickly, I make my way to him, letting the floor emphasize each of my steps with a creak. I don't bother with pretenses, so in that time, I lift the hem of my tank top over my head, uncovering my small breasts and the cool air instantly caresses my body.

I don't know how he'll react but I imagine this is what he's after, and with the weight of today still firmly weighing down on me, I want it too. I'm eager to forget it all and feel something else that is far more intoxicating to lure me into the depths of sleep.

A hiss of intake is followed by a groan of satisfaction from the man in the room, but I don't bother to look him in the eye. Leaning against the bed, I kick off the loose-fitting sweatpants, but leave on the one garment that will stay between us for the moment. With my clothes tossed carelessly on the floor of the cheap motel, I drag down the comforter that he just smoothed and crawl in.

It's not lost on me that I'm exposed, bared to a man who stays in the shadows and won't let me see him.

Something about that fact makes it even easier to do what I'm about to do next.

When I crawl on the bed, the springs give a slight protest with a soft squeak. My fingers dig into the mattress and I lean forward on my hands and knees at the top of the bed. My eyes are closed, my breathing even and I plant the barest of kisses on his hard jaw lined with stubble. He's rough against my gentleness, but something about the simple act, breaks down any wall of protest.

"Tell me it's going to be all right?" I whisper the plea, my forehead resting against his temple. If he were going to push me away, now would be the time and it's quite possibly something that will happen. An act that would destroy me.

But I would take it. I'd take it just as much as I'd take him laying me down on my stomach and fucking me raw on this bed. If he'll make everything right again, I'll let him do whatever he wants to me.

Time tortures me as I wait for what feels like forever for an answer. My eyes remain closed even when I feel him move, shifting next to me until his deft fingers slip down the curves of my side. With goosebumps following the trace of his fingertips, a shiver elicits the darkest of wants.

"It will be." His answer comes with a nip on my shoulder, a warning maybe. "You know I'm a bad man, don't you?" His warm breath trails down my shoulders like a silk sash falling from the finest of robes and all at once, he's no longer touching me.

My long lashes flutter open and I stare directly ahead at his throat. The cords in his neck tighten and the dark stubble begs me to brush the tip of my nose against it, just to feel how sharp it is. "I know exactly who you are," I whisper and although it feels true as each syllable slips out, so many questions in the back of my mind doubt my conviction.

His lips brush against mine and his smile plays against my parted lips. With the rustling of the sheets, his bottom teeth graze along my lower lip until he nips me.

The sound of shock and want mingle into a deadly concoction as I yelp, still on all fours, in only my panties. Still with my eyes closed.

His thumb brushes along my backside. "You left these on," he says and the click of the heat turning on does nothing to soothe my already heated skin.

Swallowing, I nod my head, expecting to feel him there, but he must be leaning back. My core is hot and my nipples harden. Without his touch, I could be alone on the bed for all I know, but I haven't heard the bed signal his movements.

"A touch for a touch?" he asks, giving away his position

which is only inches from me.

"Yes." The single word falls from my lips both light and heavy, with an eagerness and yet with apprehension.

His heat wraps around me as he leans in closer, the rough pad of his thumb tracing the curve of my breast and then the other. I whimper, my thighs tightening and my needs climbing higher.

"I have to warn you, Delilah," he whispers and the roughness of his stubble scrapes against the curve of my neck. It's then I can feel his bare skin against mine, my forearm pressed against his chest. Sweeping my hair to the side and exposing my back, he nips my neck and presses his hand against my upper back.

My head lowers in a bow, my ass still raised. "I'm going to take my time with you," he says and with the dizziness of a lust-filled cocktail flooding my veins I moan in response. My cheek brushes against his thigh. I'm not naïve. He's naked on the bed and his cock is near. I part my lips, willing and ready and lift my hips to accept him, but his hand bears down firmly against my shoulder blades, pushing me against the sheets.

The sound of him stroking himself is followed by the head of his cock being pressed against my lips.

"Lick it clean," he commands and my tongue darts out to taste the salty bit of precum that's waiting for me.

He strokes his cock again, his knuckles brushing against my skin.

"I'll have every bit of you," he says but it's almost as if it's a promise to himself. I take his words for what they are, a hell-bent eagerness for this man to consume me.

"Yes," I say and breathe out, feeling everything slip away. My sanity included.

It's not until he places his lips at the shell of my ear to tell me, "But you didn't beg," that I think it won't happen. He won't thrust himself inside of me and take what he wants.

I open my eyes only to stare at my own grip on the edge of the bed. The sound of his footsteps rounding the mattress is barely heard over my pounding heart.

"I told you that you'd beg for me, that you'd feel deprived without me inside of you," he says and my response is right there, so close and so wanting to be heard, but I can't speak.

"It'll be fun to play with you, though."

He keeps his promise, taking his time until I'm wrung out and begging. Even then ... he still doesn't take me.

According to him, I didn't beg fast enough, and I don't crave him enough. Yet.

Even when I whimper that I need him, it's not enough.

Chapter 13

Delilah

The ache between my thighs is unrelenting. Even in the hard chair of the interrogation room, I can barely sit without feeling him. His fingers played with me, toying and testing. Leaving me satisfied, aching, but wanting more.

My cheeks are stained with a heat that would reveal a harlot to anyone who dared to pry. The sarcastic huff notes the ridiculousness of my thoughts. Given that I'm sitting across from a man who's attempting to pin a murder on me, my focus needs to be anywhere but on Marcus.

"My mother?" I ask Detective Skov. His dark brown eyes are just slightly lighter than his thick hair. It's grown out an inch at the top and not at all tamed. Along with his overgrown stubble, on the cusp of being a beard, the man looks like he doesn't give a damn about rules and regulations. I've given him my explanation more than a handful of times now. Each time he asks nearly the same questions.

What time was that? Did you hear anyone? Did you see anything else? Can you describe... on and on. I know the tricks of the trade. He's looking for any chance to cast doubt on what I've said. To see if I'm lying.

"She's not coherent," he says and I exhale in frustration. I begged her this morning, telling her if she wanted to say something, to just cry instead. It's better for her to appear unstable than to give them an alternative version of the story.

It's not lost on me that if she slips up, if she goes weak, I'm fucked.

They'll know I lied and charges will be pressed; I'll be disbarred. It'll be the end for me.

"She wasn't coherent when I found her either," I tell Skov again. Two hours in and I'm only repeating myself now.

I can take it all day long. I don't know that the same can be said about my mother, though.

Glimpses of her disheveled state flicker in front of me and I pick under my nails rather than look back at the man I'm certain doesn't believe me. He knew my father and by association, my mother and me and my sister. Only by name, though.

"Is this a normal reaction for her?" he asks and I glare up at him.

"A normal reaction to finding her husband dead? My father,"

I say but my voice breaks and I force my eyes closed. "I'm sorry," I whisper and with both elbows on the table I hang my head in my hands. "I just ... I'm sorry," I say, apologizing again.

"For what?" he asks and if I wasn't truly destroyed from everything that's happened, I would smile at his idiocy. My story is ironclad. It's all up to my mother.

"For my shortness," I tell him and take in a steadying breath. "I'm usually more ... Talkative and approachable and ... I'm usually better." My voice cracks again as I speak and I shake my head. "I just don't understand or believe it. He can't be dead."

Believe your lies and everyone else will too. I'll never forget that phrase from Criminal Investigations 450 written on the chalkboard in a room full of expectant, soon-to-be lawyers. So long as they passed the bar.

"I should have ..." I let the statement trail off and close my eyes. My mind drifts, wandering back to the front door of the home I grew up in. My throat's tight as I remember opening it, the creak and the ominous silence that greeted me.

"It was supposed to be a girls' night," I say and my words are etched in agony as I stare up at the detective and let the pain of it all be revealed in the statement. "That's what we should be doing right now. We should be out having fun while my father attends a conference."

"As far as you know, there isn't anyone who would want your father dead."

Just as I'm about to respond by bringing up his cases from years ago or disgruntled former business partners, the door opens and Skov's partner, Gallinger, comes in. The two are complete opposites. The clean-shaven, pristine cop is at complete odds with Skov's disheveled state.

Even his polite smile and nod, plus the way he whispers to Skov, appear to be in direct conflict with the man's appearance.

"How are you, Delilah?" Gallinger asks me, pulling out a chair and sitting across from me.

"It feels like everything is coming apart," I say, making the admission because it does. And it adds to the testimony.

"You have to know how this looks," Gallinger says while gesturing with his hand, sympathy in his gaze. Skov turns, still standing and paces behind him.

"I do. Trust me, I do," I tell him and my heart beats harder, wondering what change brought him in. Did my mother say anything? *Please, God, please, I will do anything.*

"We found a note at the crime scene, did my partner tell you that?"

A flicker of hope lights with me like the small flame of an ancient furnace. "He didn't, no."

I was beginning to think Marcus never left it. Or it simply wasn't found.

The small slip of paper flitters across the table and I make great effort to only touch the plastic edges of the evidence bag it resides inside.

Bad men die.

I don't have the ability to read past the first line. My breath is stolen from me as my blood runs cold.

It's Marcus's handwriting.

He didn't try to hide it. He's pinning it on himself.

"We're running forensics," Gallinger starts to say but my head spins and a ringing in my ears drowns out his voice.

I can't breathe. I can't focus as the man speaks. Leaning forward slightly, I manage to control my breaths. In and out, in and out.

"Are you—"

I cut off his question, but I can't complete the statement as I say, "I recognize …"

My throat is tight. With my eyes closed, all I can see are the glimpses of last night.

"Recognize what?"

He had to have known I would recognize it from the cases. Analysis will point them there. To my cases. The unsolved ones that the fucking reporter brought up only a month ago.

"I got my father killed," I blurt out and I don't know why it sounds so truthful to my ears.

My hands shake at the thought of this all leading to me. Shoving them in my lap, I try to decipher Marcus's intent. Why lead them to himself? To cases I've worked on? Other than to keep me as a suspect or involved in some way.

"This is bad. I need …"

I can't think straight as my head swarms with the onslaught of coincidence.

I come into town.

The handwriting of the note matches my cold cases.

I kept my mother from coming in, who now isn't speaking.

The heat that runs along my skin is fire, but still I feel cold as ice.

"You can tell me whatever it is you need," Gallinger presses and I don't fail to notice that Skov has stopped pacing, watching me intently.

"I need Cody Walsh," I tell him and focus once again on breathing in and out. My palms press against the metal table just to feel something in this moment. "When you run forensics, you'll find they match cold cases. They're our cases from years ago. We suspected a serial killer named Marcus."

"You think he killed your father?"

"Or he's framing me." I whisper the fear at the same time a realization comes over me.

"According to the mortician, he was dead hours before you arrived," Skov says, piping up. "Gallinger filled me in a moment ago. If someone's trying to frame you—"

Gallinger cuts off Skov, saying, "Which is why it doesn't make sense that the killer waited hours after the murder before fleeing the scene when your mother says she found your father." He's quick to find a hole in the story.

I'm silent, processing the evidence they have.

The logical side of my brain pieces together my own defense first. Footage from the gas station, the toll pass stations on the highway ... there's enough to keep me away from the time of death.

A sense of calm comes over me, but only for a moment.

"My mother isn't a killer. This signature—" I start to say, but stop myself. The expectant gazes of two men searching for more stare back at me.

All I have to do is be quiet. There isn't enough evidence to convict my mother or me but there's also evidence to the contrary. Evidence that points to a killer.

But there's one little statement I want to deliberately let slip. "You think he was going to kill my mother too? He was waiting for her and then I arrived? Or was he going to kill me?"

I've never been the best actress. I can put on a show for a courtroom, but tears? Real tears? Those are hard to come by under normal circumstances, let alone this.

"If he took off when you showed up ..."

In this moment, though, it's easy to cry, mourning for my father and also shedding tears of relief for my mother. "I saved her from being killed?" I let the question fall in between us, my voice full of hope as I stare wide eyed across the table at the man who knows damn well I didn't do it. I'd bet my last dollar he's eager to get a taste of the cold cases instead of pinning my father's murder on a woman he's known for years.

With a tap on the steel table, the one detective leaves and

then the other follows.

They make me wait for at least forty minutes; the only noise to keep me company is the click of the heater turning on and then back off.

All the while I pray my mother doesn't say anything. Not a word.

She promised. I told her this morning, it was all she needed to do to keep us safe.

With the fears of the unknown by my side, I startle when the metal door opens again. Raking his hand through his unruly hair, Skov tells me I can go. And that he's sorry for my loss.

It dawns on me that he's said it more than three times now and I wonder how close he was with my father. Not enough to ask, though. Not enough to create more dialogue than needed.

"My mother?" I ask him. "Is she okay?" The thudding in my chest is heavy and refuses to go unnoticed. I only hope I can silence it.

"She needs help," he says and his thick brow furrows.

"Is my sister here? She's waiting for her? I'm sure you know she's a—"

"Yes, we're aware and your sister is on her way." Skov's lips part to say something else, his hands on his hips and I can imagine the accusations. That I shouldn't have kept my mother away last night. That I should have known she needed help.

That I'm part of the problem.

The corners of my lips are weighted down like the lead in my chest keeping me where I am until he repeats that I'm free to go.

"Thank you." My whisper grants me a nod from the man and I mentally prepare to see my sister.

Remorse isn't the word I'm feeling. It's so much more than that.

I know what she walked into alone, dreading what she'd find.

People move about me in blurs of blue and white. The phone at the front desk never stops ringing. Somehow I manage to continue moving along, taking one step after another.

I speak at the appropriate times, thanking someone at the desk as I wait in the lobby.

Through the windows of the front doors, the parking lot is clearly in view. Several cop cars are lined up in front with an assortment of random cars on the left.

I can just imagine how the red and blue lights would have hit the house late last night. How they would have shined bright against the brick. All the while, my sister was alone.

The doors open and the freezing cold air blows in. There's not a soul here I recognize.

I busy myself checking my phone. Texts from my sister, asking where I am and then others ... all that would prove my sister didn't know where I was or why my mother and myself weren't there.

Texts from Cody. He was worried. It's only then that I realize he would have gotten the news that my father was shot dead and my mother and I were missing.

The streams of texts and messages flood my soul with guilt.

What the hell is wrong with me?

There aren't enough apologies in the world, but it's what I start with: *I'm so sorry. I'm okay, I swear, just shaken up.*

It's not a lie but it feels like it is. I don't know what I'll tell him when I see him. That's the worst part.

As I'm holding my phone, a new text comes in. This time from Marcus.

I want you to meet me at an old barn.

The red barn on Cannon Road.

I respond:

I know it. Why there?

My father used to meet his friends there to work on tractors and other machinery. It was a hobby of his. I don't have time to mourn the memories because two things happen at once.

My sister cries out, a purse dangling from the crook of her arm and her coat hanging from her shoulder as she runs toward me.

"Baby," my mother calls out behind me and the two pass just to my left, hugging each other with tears streaking down their faces. I stand there alone, feeling my phone go off.

Glancing down, I see it's both Marcus and Cody.

I can't even begin to think of a response to Cody. I'm depleted and I have a pile of lies to explain to him, none of which I want to ... and a million apologies on top of that. I don't know what to say to him and that's become a staple in our relationship.

Again the doors open and all that hugs me in this moment is the chill of the autumn wind.

"Cady cat," I say and I don't know why the weakly spoken nickname comes out like that. I haven't called her that in years.

Slowly, her grip loosens on my mother and she peers at me, the kohl liner around her eyes making them look even larger than they are. She readjusts her black wool coat before pulling me into a firm hug.

My grip on her is tighter than I consciously allow. I can't let her go even if I wanted to.

"It's going to be okay," she tells me, but I'm not sure I believe it.

Chapter 14

Marcus
Nineteen Years Ago

He looks just like the rest of them. There's nothing at all distinctive about his features. Maybe the reddened cheeks would set him apart if it were any other day. But with the festival, all the adults with beers in oversized plastic cups have red cheeks.

He smiles too, just like them. His isn't as white and polished, though. Years of smoking took its toll. Maybe his skin is slightly more yellow too, although it's hard to tell from this far back.

Slipping my hands into my jean pockets, I keep my distance, slipping down the cracked sidewalk between rows of people cheering on the green floats. My shoulder brushes against the brick wall and occasionally there's a bump from someone stepping back or trying to get around the crowd.

"Hey, watch it."

"Oh, I'm sorry, kid."

"Where's your mom?"

I ignore them all, keep my head down and smile. I've found if I just point ahead and keep walking, no one stops me. They don't bother to get a response before turning their back to me and carrying on.

It's warmer down here than it is at the barn. It took me three days to get here although it's only hours if you take the highway. I learned that from my last hitchhike.

From the barn and my safe place, all the way to a different small town I grew up in, is only three hours away. Three long hours down the highway carved into the mountains.

The next float strolls by and this time the man stops. He shouts something, cupping his hands around his mouth to call out across the street. His smile broadens and the cheers get louder as the music does. Everything is so damn loud, but it's silent just the same.

It doesn't matter; it doesn't mean anything.

For Harold it's just another reason to drink and then get in his car.

I wish I could steal his car from him when I'm done. That's a regret I have. But my teacher, the monster he is, would never do such a thing. He doesn't take trophies. That's a rule.

Even if I could steal the car and take it from him, it's not like I could drive it.

So for now, sneaking onto trains and in the back of trucks to get back home will have to do. But I'd be damned if I didn't admit the trunk would be a good place to sleep at night. A closed-off, locked space ... I can only imagine.

A cool breeze blows by and I instinctively look for the stairways down to the stores. They block the wind too and when the stores are closed, bundling up in the corner and hiding behind a trash bag works quite well. They can't see me. So long as they can't see me, then everything is all right.

"You okay?" a woman asks as she stumbles into me, her sharp red nails digging into my shoulder as she braces herself against me. I get the idea that her instinct was to keep me upright, but she staggers in her high heels.

Her lashes are dark and long and there are little diamonds at the corners of her eyes. "Little dude, you shouldn't be out here all alone," she tells me and looks past me.

She seems like one of the good ones. One of the ones who need protecting. She's so much taller than me. Pretty bird. That's what the man would call her. But only once he was done with her.

"You lost?" she asks when I don't answer. I smile up at her, shaking my head and tell her I'm just going home. She smiles back. "Be careful, cutie."

The short interaction almost makes me lose him. I can't lose sight of him. Not today. Today is the day it has to happen. A numbness pricks along my skin as I follow Harold around the corner, quickening my steps and slipping through the crowd.

Harold disappears into a liquor store, one he's been in a number of times. I bide my time, finding a rock and carving something into the concrete. It won't last, just like the promise I make with the stone won't either.

Kids play with rocks outside of stores. No one looks twice.

With the parade, the noise and the crowds to slip back into, the timing is perfect for my first.

And Harold has to be the first.

Harold has a habit. It's a bad one that he's yet to learn from. He drinks, then gets into his '86 Ford and drives home. His brother, a senator, got him off this last time. The charges suddenly disappeared, as did his sobriety test results. The scandal was all over the news. And even though there isn't a damn thing distinctive about Harold, I knew him. I recognized him.

Because he's the man who took my parents away. He caused the accident; he set all of this into motion. He should be my first.

The moment I saw his picture in the crinkled newspaper that reeked of the coffee it was stained with, it all made sense.

It was meant to be this way.

He took my parents, and that led to everything. He started it all and who I was before will end with him. Only then can I truly be Marcus.

The bad guys always lose and he is a bad guy. Even if he smiles. Even if his brother is a senator. Even if tonight he decided to walk instead of getting into his car. His victims don't get to decide anything anymore.

If he hadn't done it again, if it hadn't been in the papers I scavenged while rummaging in the dumpsters that lined the alley hours away from here, it never would have occurred to me. I wouldn't have chosen him. But he did do it again and they let him go. They gave him another chance, but that's not fair when the man he killed didn't get another chance.

Harold is a bad man and his time is up.

A numbness pricks down my arm, my fingers twitching for the cheap blade I found last week. The very day my plan came together. It's funny how things all align when you have a plan. How the pieces fall into place and it's so much easier to sleep, to move forward.

His death is my purpose.

As we round the corner of the liquor store, the parade falls behind us. With a bottle wrapped in a brown paper bag, it seems he's given up on the beer and moved on to something harder. I've watched Harold for nearly a week and his routine is simple. He leaves his home around noon. He wears jeans stained with old paint. He goes to the bar down Fifth Street and when they kick him out, he goes to the liquor store he just came out of.

Then he goes back down to Fifth but he takes the alley. It's so he can piss on the wall or the cars in the parking lot behind the bar. He's only done it twice, but his rough laugh that echoes late at night indicates he truly enjoys it. It's just as much a part of his nightcap as the bottle of gin he's got gripped in his right hand.

I'm grateful he's gone down this way tonight. I don't know why he's already headed down the back path, given that he wasn't even at the bar for long today and left to see the parade. Old habits die hard, I suppose.

Back here it's quieter, but the music still filters through. I keep to the left, next to the trash cans and look down at the old stone that's unrepaired and the rubble of concrete that was used to fill the gaps years ago.

My heart races, moving so much faster than my footsteps in the worn sneakers that don't quite fit. Everything feels hot, even though I'm aware I'll be freezing tonight, wherever I lie down to rest. The blood rushes in my ears so loud I can barely hear him.

His jacket rustles when I tap his shoulder. I have to look up to do it, my neck craning because he's a larger man, rotund from drinking and not doing a damn thing else. When he turns I'm quick to hit him in his groin, catching him off guard to steal his wallet.

Chase me down the alley, my inner voice prays. My sneakers squeak as I run farther to the left, farther away from the couple kissing past the dumpsters at the start of the busy street.

So we can be alone.

"Little shit." His groan fills the smaller space, the alley that leads down to an old row of homes built for the steel mill. You can barely fit a bike through this alley. I remember when my brother did it, though.

With everything raging inside of me, I don't count on the tears or how my gaze becomes glossy at the memory.

Cody had me on the back of his bike, and he was able to ride down an alley just like this one. I remember how scared I was that he was going to hit the wall or that his handlebars would catch the side of a brick. I shouldn't be thinking of him right now. I lose myself, my focus, I lose everything remembering how I held on so tight to him. Stopping in my tracks, right in the middle, the man curses behind me and grabs my shoulder.

I don't even recall my hand wrapping around the blade, but when I strike him in the gut, once then twice, that's when I realize what I've done and that I'm still here. I'm not back with Cody, holding on to a small bag of candy.

I'm not there at all. I'm holding a bloody blade and looking up at a man who fails to say anything.

Harold looks older than the picture in the paper when I look up. His skin is a little more yellow too, and more wrinkled than the paper. The shock in his gaze was also absent then.

I hesitate for only a moment when his wide eyes look down at me. He stumbles back just slightly and I stand facing him in the narrow alley, his wallet in one hand and the blade in the other.

My heart is still racing, but he's more disoriented than I am. And I'm the one with the plan. He swallows thickly before calling out for help.

The man's on his ass, scooting backward. He's trying to get away, but what's done is done. There's sorrow and sympathy, but it's odd how it comes, how it's because it's like Cody's watching me. He wouldn't want this, but Cody's not here and he'll never know.

Everything speeds up then. I only hesitate because he's watching me. The moment Harold turns his head to look behind him, maybe to cry out for help again, I strike. Eating up the short distance between us with long strides and slicing his throat.

Once, twice, and a third time.

It gushes at first, hot and bubbly. It's different than what I've seen in the barn.

He clutches at his throat, trying to speak.

I don't tell him why. I wonder if when we die, we can still ponder things. I hope not. I want the things I think about to rest once I'm gone.

I watch him, and make sure he's gone. It doesn't take long. It's so much faster and simpler than I thought it would be.

A breeze goes through the alley and my face is cold. Streaks of what feels like ice make me shiver involuntarily until I brush away the tears. They're unexpected.

I clean off the knife on his shirt before dropping it down a sewer. The last act that involves Harold has to do with his wallet. I collect the cash and pocket it. Only forty-three dollars. Then I drop the wallet down the grates along the street too.

The white noise fades fast and I can hear the parade again, like nothing happened. Picking up a stick, I trail it along the mortar between the bricks of the building. Because that's what kids do, they like sticks and rocks and keeping to themselves.

I keep walking and I don't look back. Instead I think about Cody and how that was the only time we rode down that alley. How when we went down it, I couldn't wait to try on my own. I was going to have my own bike soon and I was going to do it too.

I don't hear anyone scream like I thought I would. Watching the parade from the end of the street where it's taped off I wait, but no one ever screams.

The sirens come and no one wants to part to let them through.

It's for the better outcome.

It's for all the pretty little birds.

Chapter 15

Delilah

I was never adventurous. I didn't want to go play outside. My father locked the door once after telling my sister and me to go on the front porch. He yelled through the closed door to go play and turned his back to us.

I suppose telling us we couldn't stay inside all day during summer got old, so he resorted to kicking us out. When the streetlights came on and dinner was on the table, we were finally allowed back in. But kids were supposed to be outside playing when the sun was out. Luckily, I almost always had a book to keep me occupied.

Inhaling the fresh smell of the forests to the left and the hints of hay from the field to the right, I don't know why I didn't play out here more. It's peaceful.

The field didn't scare me like it did my sister. She said she could get lost in the long rows of corn and that freaked her out.

She hated it out here. I remember her, so much taller than me, with her arms crossed over her chest in her favorite blue jean jacket. She'd rather lose at hide-and-seek than take one step into that cornfield. I don't know why it spooked her like it did, but I love it out here.

The red barn always looked beat down to me back then and the years haven't been kind to it now.

I wonder what Marcus knows. There's no such thing as coincidence when it comes to him. There's a reason he brought me back here to the place I know my father used to hide away in.

When my mother and he were fighting, he'd always take off to help Mr. Dave fix up the old machines. There's more than a time or two I can recall Mom hunched over the sink, gripping the counter and pretending not to cry when I stepped into the kitchen after hearing the argument from upstairs.

She'd wipe away the tears with her back to me, and dry her hands on the flannel towel that hung from the cabinet below.

"Clean yourself up. It's almost time for breakfast." It wasn't always breakfast she'd say; the meals were interchangeable and all corresponded to the time of day.

I can picture it so clearly, the same tearstained cheeks she had only yesterday with her hair up in a silk wrap and not a dress to be seen for days.

When they fought, the kitchen was her safe place. This barn was his.

"What does it mean to you?" Marcus's voice calls out and it scares me, causing me to stagger a step back. He's in jeans and a hoodie, maybe ten feet away under the shade of an old pine tree. Leaning against it, with his hands in his pockets, he looks relaxed which is at odds with everything I know about him.

"What does what mean? What does what mean to me?" I have to speak up a little louder than comfortable for him to hear me. The gray clouds part in the muted sky and as Marcus makes his way to me, I see his face easily enough.

Sucking in a breath, I turn to stare at the barn, pretending I didn't just see his features plain as day.

"Don't tell anyone you saw me," he commands although it sounds like a question. His charming smirk looks far too boyish on him. Maybe it's the pale blue eyes and faint wrinkles around them that give him his boy-next-door appeal. His dirty blond hair tousled by the wind makes him appear all soft, but his jaw is hard and his features severe the moment he tilts his head. "You understand that, don't you?"

More than anything, he looks just like Cody.

"You're his brother ... you're Chris—"

"Don't," he says, cutting me off and I silence myself, chewing on the inside of my cheek. My pulse races and my heart hammers. They found dental records. The world thought him dead. My mind filters through the tragic tale. If he's Christopher, Cody's brother ...

"I can see the wheels turning," Marcus says, coming up beside me. I stay facing the barn, wrapping my arms around myself as the wind blows.

"Is that right?" I ask him, peeking up but quickly looking away. He's leaner than Cody; I can't help but to compare every bit of him to his brother.

"Don't think about it."

"I'm not sure what you mean."

"Everything eludes you today ..." Marcus says and disappointment is evident in his tone.

"What did you mean by your question?" I ask him. He stands beside me, his arm almost touching mine. He's taller than me but on the hill like we are, he's even taller and he practically towers over me.

Power radiates from him. Even the air seems to bend around him.

"This barn. What does it mean to you?" he asks and I shrug.

"It's an old place and ... I used to come out here sometimes, but not a lot." I almost bring up my father, but I choke on his name.

"If they knocked it down, tore it to pieces?"

"It wouldn't matter to me," I tell him, and peek up questioningly. "Why would you think it would?"

"What about your family home? If they took it apart brick by brick?"

"You could take it ... I'd still be okay." My mind spins with questions, wondering why he thought this barn would mean anything at all compared to my family house. Is it because of my father?

"Is there no place you thought of as home?" he asks me genuinely and when he does, his arm brushes against mine, offering the barest of warmth.

"That tree over there," I say, motioning toward an old oak tree near the center of the field. "That's the wishing tree."

"It grants wishes?" His smirk is heard just as it is easily seen. It warms me, though, something deep down I can't explain.

"When we were kids, some boy on the bus said you had to run through the field late at night and climb it to wish on the stars or else your wishes wouldn't come true."

"I never heard that one," Marcus says and my heart flickers.

"I think in most towns it's wishing on shooting stars." I turn away from him and stare at the auburn leaves, mixed with hues of gold as I add, "But here we had that tree."

"So if it were to be chopped down?" Marcus asks.

"I'd be all right. None of this ..." I almost tell him it's not the place, it's the people. But I bite my tongue at the thought that he'd threaten to take them away.

"You'd break. At some point, we all break."

"I feel like I already have and it has nothing to do with where I grew up." I don't hide my vulnerability.

"It has everything to do with that, and trust me Delilah, you are far from broken yet."

There's an eerie air that surrounds us, almost feeling like a push and a pull at the same time. A warning and a promise.

"Is that why you wanted to meet?" I ask him. After last night, I don't know what to think.

"To ask you what a barn means to you?" he says and huffs a humorless laugh. "No, that's not why."

He doesn't offer any explanation and the wind blows gently between us. Moving the hair out of my face, I wait for him to say more, but he doesn't.

"Thank you for the note." Marcus is silent, staring off at the old tree. A crease is in the center of his forehead.

"It's your handwriting," I say, prompting him to say more.

"I'm aware."

"Well … how?" I can't get the question out; it feels very much like I'm stepping over his boundaries.

"That's not something for you to worry your pretty little head about." The mannerism in which he speaks sounds so much like Cody too. I haven't noticed it until now, maybe because he's never been this casual before. Or maybe it's because I can see his lips now. The same lips I've kissed.

"You and Cody?" I can't help myself as my heart breaks, splitting down the center. "Does he know?"

"I don't want him here." He clears his throat, hardening his voice and that depth of darkness comes back to his cadence as he adds, "I mean, I don't want to speak about him. Not here."

"I'm sorry I brought it up." A hint of fear simmers in my blood.

"I thought maybe it would help me, to see you here."

"Help with what?" I dare to ask.

I don't know why, but there's a deep-seated pain that rests in his gaze. I wish I could stop it, erase it from all existence. It doesn't belong there.

In a single blink it's gone, replaced by a narrow gaze and a teasing smirk. The air shimmers and I nearly second-guess what I saw. "There's no one here …" His voice is deep and seems to rumble from his chest. "I could do anything I want to you."

I know only days ago, the statement would elicit more fear than anything else. As he looks down at me, like a hunter at his prey, there isn't anything I feel other than want.

He makes me want more than I ever thought possible. It's all the teasing. It has to be the way he plays with me.

As if that is something that should turn me on. I'm a foolish girl and so very aware of it when I ask him, "And what is it that you want to do to me?"

Thump, *thump*, the thrumming in my veins provides such little heat compared to what I know he could give me. "It's more …" he starts but then huffs a laugh and asks a question instead. "Would you kiss me still?"

"What?" Nothing he says tonight makes any sense. Not with what I currently know.

"Now that you don't need me?"

Is that what caused the pain in his gaze? He's truly mad.

"Do you want to kiss me?" he asks bluntly as I stand there, feeling as if I'm nothing beneath him and wondering how he could see me as anything at all.

"Yes." I answer without thinking.

"How badly?"

My heart beats madly as I see the desperation in his cold eyes. On tiptoes, I kiss him. No thought at all, just a desire, a wish come true that didn't take crossing a barren field and climbing up an old tree. A real kiss between a man and a woman. It's tender, but quickly deepens. His hand splays against my back and braces me there.

Ever so slowly, I reach up, my hand resting on his collarbone and the other sneaking up.

It's over far too quickly at the sound of tires in the distance, just beyond the tree line where the backroad is and where my car is parked.

The gentle moment vanishes, and without a goodbye, Marcus leaves, stalking toward the barn. I'd follow, but my name is carried with the wind.

"Delilah," Cody's voice calls out followed by the sound of

a car door shutting.

Fuck, fuck, fuck.

I'm sure he can tell something's off—I can see it in the way he strides to me, at first deliberate and then slowed. My breathing is erratic and my mind races not knowing how to pick up the pieces of where I left off with Cody Walsh.

So much has happened since I met him in a darling coffee shop with a soft goodbye kiss. Too much to explain and far too complicated.

"Delilah," he says and relief is evident in my name on his lips.

"Cody …I …" I struggle to put anything into words, pulling at my sleeve and meeting him halfway to where he is. The barn is at my right, the field at my back and in front of me, is a man who stares down with both worry and devotion.

"How did you know to find me here?" I ask rather than digging deep. I've just kissed his brother, a man who helped me help my mother get away with murder.

The confessions threaten to tumble out and smother me even in the fresh air.

"Your cell phone," Cody says and his expression wrinkles with questions of his own.

"Right, right," I say, turning away from him as the clouds return and the gray sky morphs to dark shades of blue in the skyline. It's darker sooner this time of year.

There's never been a time in my life where I caught sight of Cody and felt what I feel now. This feeling like I should be running and hiding from him is completely alien but still it seems like the right thing to do. The dread that seeps into my blood, weighing everything down like lead, keeps me planted right where I am.

"I'm sorry I didn't call and I didn't answer …" I push out the apology, needing it to be heard in its sincerity. "You didn't deserve to worry."

"Don't be. I know why …" He's calm, far too calm. As if he knows. My heart hammers and I wonder what information he's gathered.

There's a silence between us, and an uncomfortable prick at the back of my neck. I'm certain that somewhere, Marcus watches.

I want to tell him. When Cody looks at me like he is, with his hands slipping into his jean pockets, his Henley blowing slightly in the wind but still firm on his broad shoulders, I want to wrap my fingers in the light gray fabric and pull him closer. I want to confide in my friend and be held by my lover.

I don't deserve an ounce of that want. I've ruined it; I've sacrificed us … even if he doesn't know.

"I'm sorry about your father," he finally speaks. Glancing behind him, for only a moment, I see my father standing there at the entrance to the barn, locking it and telling me this is no place for kids. To go away unless I want to work.

His voice is so clear in my memory. My eyes prick and that could be the wind, it could be the unforgiving breeze. But my throat getting tight isn't from the weather.

"Thank you," I say in a nearly inaudible whisper. "You followed me here to give me your condolences?"

"Don't do that," he says, scolding my sarcasm, but it's not in a superior way. There's only pain that lays in his words.

"I just … I'm not well right now," I say, giving him the honest answer. I don't want Marcus watching us. Not when Cody doesn't know it. Not when I just kissed him. "I'm not doing well."

"We need to talk about this."

"We don't, though," I say and shake my head in denial.

"They brought me on the case." His tone is firm when he answers.

And for a moment I pause.

"The case? My father's murder?" That's what he wants to talk about … not us? I deserve the pain that grips me and tears me into two. "I don't want to talk about this right now …"

"We can't wait on this, Delilah." Cody doesn't let up and I know just looking at him that he's not going to let me walk away and hide. He's not going to back off, not a single step. It's an indescribable pain, knowing that there is no way to go back and how badly I've hurt him and ruined us.

I don't want him to know. If I could keep it from him and

let him down easy, it would be best, wouldn't it?

"There are questions ..." he continues and I have to close my eyes, taking in a steadying breath. With everything between us, the tension, the disappointment ... the last thing I want to think about is my father's death. A snide voice hisses, *it's murder* in the back of my mind. *Your father's murder, not death.*

"Can we talk about it another time?" I ask although I don't wait for a response and turn away from him, wanting to get to my car. With the sun hidden behind the clouds, the autumn turned brutal without any warning.

Cody's quick to grab my wrist. It's not so much that it hurts or that it jostles me. The firm grasp only keeps me from moving away, but it's the desperation in his touch that has my eyes pinned to his and my breath stolen.

My heart races.

"I fucked up, Delilah," he says just beneath his breath. His ever-confident tone is shaken and his gaze falls before mine. Glancing behind me, an act that sends a chill down my spine, knowing that Marcus could be and probably is watching.

My shoulders shudder with the cold breeze as I wrench my hand away, although my flats are firmly planted where they stand.

"I know he spoke to you," Cody whispers even though, to his knowledge, there's no one here to eavesdrop. The breeze blows through the tree leaves and another chill runs through me.

Ever the gentleman, Cody removes his jacket, but he doesn't lay it across my shoulders. Instead he offers it as if he's not sure that I'll take it.

In a formfitting Henley, snug on his shoulders, he looks back at me with a softness in his blue eyes. "Please, even if you're angry." My pulse weakens watching him struggle in front of me. His eyes are rimmed with red and the chill has bitten his cheeks, turning them a pink hue to match the tip of his nose.

Reaching out to grab it, I take a half step closer to him and slip his jacket around my shoulders, even if it is far too oversized for me. The warmth is immediate, blanketing me as if it's safe now. As If nothing can hurt me beneath the shield of this man.

With his hands in his jean pockets, Cody says, "I know he spoke to you and I've lied. I've kept things from you."

The world blurs behind him.

"There are so many reasons I can't—I couldn't." He's quick to correct himself but that mistake forces him to heave in a flustered breath.

"Just tell me the truth," I plead with him.

"That's what I want to do, Delilah." His eyes hold nothing but sincerity. "I want to tell you everything."

Chapter 16

Marcus
Sixteen Years Ago

Some things never change. Like the streetlamp on Parkway Avenue coming on before the rest of the lights in the vicinity. Or the bench outside of the hardware store being fully occupied with high school kids. The roll of wheels from skateboards and the chatter bring back memories.

Back then, they were the big kids. Now I'm around their age, maybe older.

The keys clang in my hand as I twirl them around my fingers. The small shop area used to be bustling this late at night. I noticed the new mall down the highway coming in and wondered if it would affect the stores here.

Maybe some things do change.

I don't even know what I'm doing here.

Things are tedious upstate and I may have been a little reckless. While the heat dies down, it's best to get away. I could have gone anywhere, though. Nothing explains why I ended up here in the town I grew up in.

With a few hundred dollars in my pocket, and a car to stay in, I could go just about anywhere. So long as I don't get caught, I'm golden. The fake license, the fake storylines—it's all worked out well for me these last two years. It's easy to make necessary acquaintances when you know people. And more importantly, when they know your name.

It's best they don't see my face, though, or ever meet me in person. I'm far too young. I've had to kill too many men already for their arrogance and laughter when they see me. I can't risk a damaged reputation because some old fuck doesn't know what's good for him.

Like I said, it's tedious. And I needed to get away for a while.

The jingling stops, the clatter of skateboards hitting the sidewalk and the rev of engines at the streetlight behind me turning to white noise. None of it makes any noise at all when I stare straight ahead. Because I see them. Cody's still living with my uncle. A smirk kicks my lips up as I think, I might be as tall as him now.

They walk side by side, Cody right at Uncle Myron's height. Although it's obvious he's younger. He should be headed to college. I saw online and on social media. He got into a few good schools but he hasn't decided yet where he wants to go.

He's got a girlfriend too and a job at my uncle's friend's construction site.

He wants to be a cop, though. My brother ... a cop.

Shaking my head, I wave off the woman who stopped to ask if I'm all right. "Fine," I answer her and her brow wrinkles. Before I can head out, following down the path Cody and Uncle Myron just took, she asks me, "Are you a Walsh?"

I've practiced my expressions a million times. It's a way to keep people from knowing what you're thinking. Or vice versa to control a situation. Still, I feel my own expression fall.

Just like how the feeling of dread drops into the pit of my stomach.

I don't recognize her. Not in the least. The tight white curls that stop above her shoulders may have been dark brown locks long ago. I don't know who she is, but with that questioning look in her eyes, I can see that she remembers me.

"No ma'am," I say, putting on a slight Southern accent. "Have a good evening."

With the dull thud in my chest and the numbing tingling on my skin, I head off with my hands in my pockets and search out my brother. I only look back once and the woman's still standing there, a bag in one hand and a cane in the other. People move on, people stop talking, and people get forgotten.

Maybe it's selfish for me not to want to forget Cody, when I'm doing everything I can for everyone to forget who

I used to be.

He has everything going for him. I've kept an eye out for years. It helps me sleep at night to just check in.

He doesn't need someone like me. He's going to be a cop, for fuck's sake. Melancholy drifts into the darkness of my mind when I turn the corner and no one's there. Hell, maybe one day he'll arrest me.

I wonder if he'd know it's me. I don't see how he would. I'm dead and long gone and he's the man everyone thought he'd become.

"Hey kid," I say, tilting my chin up at one of the smaller kids a good bit away from the others. In his striped shirt and baggy black pants with more pockets than anyone would know what to do with, he's trying to do some trick on a skateboard that looks far too big for him. "Want to earn a dollar?"

"Yeah," he says with his eyes wide.

"Would you go in there and get me a bag of jerky?" I ask him, digging out five dollars and handing it over.

"You just want me to buy you jerky?" he says, hesitantly staring at the money I'm holding out for him to take.

"It only costs a few bucks, bet it'll be a bit more than a dollar left over." His hazel eyes peer up at me and then shine with delight when I add, "And it's all yours."

"You got it, mister," he says, picking up the skateboard at the same time as he snatches the five.

It would be easy to just buy the damn thing myself, but this is how you meet people. It's how you build trust. And no one suspects kids. They don't know what's going on. They don't talk to people and if they do, they aren't taken seriously.

Maybe I shouldn't set myself up here, not when some woman I don't even know recognizes me.

I'm just ... checking in and then I'll be gone.

Back to the barn where I belong.

Chapter 17

Cody
Nine Years Ago

This town is haunted. Or there's someone following me. There isn't any other explanation for it.

At first I thought it was nerves from starting this job. Working murder cases and being called out to dead body after dead body would take a toll mentally on anyone.

But I keep seeing him. I swear I see the same man over and over again.

I swallow thickly, the folded note tucked safely in my hand as I sit at the busy bar. I used to think I saw him back home too. Every so often, a block or two behind me. More than once I've chased after a figure that ran when I called out his name.

The grief counselors said it was in my head. But to follow

me here?

I'm either haunted by him, or he's here.

"Another?" the waitress asks and I nod my head, adding a *yes, please.* The first four beers should be enough. I'm already hearing his voice again and remembering the last time I said goodbye. It wasn't good enough.

The regret is what I need to let go of. That's what the therapist said, but if I let go of it, then I let go of him.

I could feel myself on the edge of crying. It wasn't fair he was going to live with our aunt and I was going to our Uncle Myron's. The lawyers didn't want us split up, but the judge said it was for the best. We were to stay with family and that meant we were going separate ways.

So when Christopher hugged me and he started crying like I wanted to, I had to be strong. Dad would have wanted me to. I made it quick and then I ripped him off of me, telling him I'd see him soon and to act right.

I've carried that guilt and regret with me for as long as I can remember. As I sit here in the bar, it overwhelms everything and that should be my cue to stop drinking, but the beers come easy and the memories ... I don't want to let go of them.

"A love letter?" the waitress jokes, nodding her head at the note in my hand as the beer hits the bar top. I only huff a laugh and she gets the hint, taking off before I feel obligated to say anything more.

A small boy's laughter resonates in the back of my mind, complete with a picture of my little brother smiling as he makes fun of me: *a love letter.*

He wouldn't be a child any longer, though. And whoever wrote this, isn't my brother. The second part of that statement is the one I'm hung up on.

I was a little messy with this one but you'll help me, won't you?

I've done what I can to help you and I know you want to help me too.

Now's your chance. I've been looking forward to this. For so long. I miss you.

He didn't sign a name. The note is written in blue ink and the handwritten font itself is unique. All the letter *A*s are written two different ways. When I looked it up in the system, searching for a match so I could come up with a suspect list, I was shocked at the number of hits it got.

All over the tristate area and for all sorts of crime. From petty theft five years ago, to money laundering cases that led to murder and a wanted serial killer in this part of Pennsylvania. There was even a hit from an apology note dating back almost a decade ago. A brick was thrown into a small sandwich shop and food stolen. The apology note is what tipped me off. Christopher used to say sorry that way. *I know it was wrong and I'll make it right.*

He always said that right after he said he was sorry. Always. The deep-down gut feeling just won't let that go. The detectives working the case left a synopsis that sends a chill down my spine.

They suspected a young boy at first, or a very uneducated adult because of the grammar and spelling. As the crimes increased in intensity and number, they were able to narrow down the criminal profile. It was textbook how the crimes progressed.

Now he's a serial killer. And a shadow who's followed me for years.

The beer slips from my hand, luckily landing with a clank and then bottoming out on the tabletop. With a glance over my right shoulder, then the left, I pull my shit together.

My brother would have been that old then. My brother would fit a description of a young white male in his early twenties.

"I didn't tell anyone," I say then clear my throat, sitting at the very end of a bar in Delilah's hometown. "I was just starting, only a month in. And I thought …" I pause to take in a deep breath, inhaling the scent of pale ales and IPAs from the draft the bartender pours. The mug is tilted and the foam spills over to the sound of another classic rock song coming on.

"At first I thought I … I didn't know what to think. It was a hunch and I thought maybe I just wanted him to be alive, you know?" The men in the back make a ruckus when someone hits the dartboard. We're surrounded by clatter and barflies, but I've never felt more alone.

Until Delilah leans forward, her hands wrapped around an untouched glass of white wine. She peeks up at me and then scoots closer, her right side brushing up against mine.

"You wanted him to be alive."

"It was more than that ... the way he said things ... they were different for me than they were for the other notes and they hit on memories.

"It was like he wanted me to know, but he never outright said it.

"I thought it was all in my head ... that the suspect was a surrogate or worse, was playing me."

"I was there," Delilah whispers, his gaze turning to the sweet liquid in the wineglass. She runs her finger around the rim of it. "You never told me."

"I didn't tell anyone," I say and my excuse sounds just like what it is. An excuse. Her small hand is gentle as she rests it on my thigh and rubs back and forth in a soothing motion. Her lips part but she doesn't say anything. Neither of us does for a moment until she takes a sip of wine and then leans closer to me.

"You were hurting, you were scared and didn't know who you could trust or if what you were doing was the right thing." She adds to my excuses, my reasoning for going along with it back then.

"Maybe it worked like that at first. But then ... he'd ... he'd set people up to go down and give me leads on them."

"You worked together?" she asks and I nod. The truth is begging to be spoken aloud finally. All those cold cases. All those men who disappeared. I knew it was coming. I knew Marcus wanted to interfere and I let it happen.

Instead of bringing any of that to light, I lift my beer to my lips and take a swig.

"I should have told you." I nod my head, agreeing with myself. "We were partners."

"I could have told our superiors. It sounds crazy, Cody. You sound crazy even now when ... when I believe you," Delilah says and glances at her wine, then back at me. Her plump lips are a dark shade of red that complements her warm umber skin.

It hurts to watch her, knowing she's conflicted and that she's hiding from me. She doesn't know I know. I can see how much it kills her. Every time she slips beside me, letting her gentle soul be seen, she pulls back, stares at her wine and the sadness overwhelms her.

It's not fair to her that it happened this way.

"I was afraid to trust him at first ..." I trail off, remembering the instincts pulling me in all directions. She's got to be going through the same. I can be there for her, though.

An older man rises beside us, making his way to the back

probably to relieve himself. With him gone, there's no one surrounding us. The place is only half-full and most of the people are at the other end of the bar where the flat screens are playing football.

"I know ... I know he kissed you." I let the confession slip out without looking back at her. Even though I can feel her gaze pierce into me, begging me to look back at her, I continue, wanting to get it all out so we can start over. So we can start fresh now with no secrets or lies between us. "I know he traded ... he plays games ..." I suspected something was up when I started to receive fewer texts from him, but the ones from two days ago when she never texted and her father was found dead spelled out everything.

He was with her, protecting her and he didn't want me to worry.

It's like stepping into an ice bath remembering the message he sent. If I hadn't been stopped at that red light, I swear to God I would have crashed.

"That's why you backed away from me?" I ask her, finally taking a peek down at Delilah and finding those big brown eyes staring up at me. They're bathed in insecurity and begging for forgiveness.

Her lips are parted and her breathing is staggered.

"It's because he stepped in, not because of something I did?" Even as I speak the last part, I know that's not all true. It's because he told her first. I should have told her. The moment I wanted her in my bed every night. The moment he came into my place and scared her. I should have told her everything.

"Cody," she whispers, emotion drenching my name.

"I can deal with that. As long as you still want me," I admit to her and feel the ache of needing her, truly and deeply needing her to forgive me and care for me again. I waited so long to make a move and it's because of my brother. The way he spoke about her ... I thought he wanted her and if I kissed her ...

I thought he'd moved on and I thought wrong.

"Cody. I did more than kiss him," she says. Her confession is spoken in a tight voice and the nervous exhale that follows adds to her uneasy posture. She won't even look at me, staring across the bar at an empty seat instead.

He did more than kiss her? The betrayal and jealousy are felt instantly, deep and primal. Licking my bottom lip, I stare straight ahead and attempt to take another swig of beer, but I can't. I'd rather throw it at the back wall. Every muscle coils inside of me.

If he thinks I'll let him use her like he used me, he's dead fucking wrong. Brother or not, I'll kill him for bringing her into this. He said he was protecting her. That doesn't mean fucking her.

After a moment, I swallow thickly, take a drink and tell her, although I still stare at the back wall as I do, "If I had told you … you wouldn't have."

"You don't know that and this isn't your fault. I made that decision."

She doesn't know who she's dealing with. She doesn't know the lengths that Marcus is willing to go to. Every warning screams at the back of my throat, yet there's only ringing in my ears when I peer down at her.

"If you want me to go, I won't. I'm not going to just let you go either," I finally tell her and her reaction at my admission is everything. From the soft inhale and slight lean forward, to the way her hands seem to inch across her lap to get closer to me. I haven't lost her yet.

"I won't lose you," I tell her and I promise myself. My pulse picks up and the heat between us is coming back. "I don't know what would happen to me if I did."

Chapter 18

Delilah

Cadence's place is small, but plenty big enough for the three of us. She's got a corner lot for her condo and Mom's been on the porch outside almost all day. I keep checking on her and so does Cadence.

Clicking send on the email, my stomach sinks and the sip of coffee doesn't help the sickness that's settled there. Claire's agreed to let me stay here rather than come in for an immediate evaluation as the board demanded. I'm on leave and they can't mandate that I be brought in on a whim when I haven't been formally charged with anything.

I have two weeks and then I need to follow procedures. Starting with a psych evaluation.

Even Aaron, the secretary, sent an email asking if I was

all right. I'm more than certain the office, and probably the whole courthouse, is buzzing with gossip of my father's death and my possible involvement given the note that was left.

Miller and Judge Malden also sent their condolences via flowers to the office. Aaron provided me with pictures. The prick that travels along my arms as I close my laptop on the kitchen counter accompanies the questions. So many questions but the main one being, do they suspect I was involved?

Sometimes we let our minds get away from us, and I remind myself of that. There's no way they suspect me. My mother, though? It's almost always the partner when a husband or wife is murdered. Almost always.

"I swear, it never stops." My sister's already speaking, her voice coming into the kitchen before she's even down the stairs. Her heels click as she rounds the banister. "I'll only be gone for an hour, though," she tells me even though she's staring into her purse, digging for her keys most likely. She adds, "tops," and like I suspected, her keys dangle from her hands.

Her hair is perfection, with thick natural curls that shine down to her shoulder blades. A black pencil skirt and a cream blouse are classically professional, yet on her body they could look scandalous.

"They really called you in two days after?" I ask her and she lets out a sigh of frustration before slinging the black leather hobo bag onto her shoulder.

"It's not them, it's my patients."

Guilt rides down on me. "I'm the workaholic, not you. Maybe you would say I'm projecting because work is what I wish I were doing."

"No," she says and then leans forward, giving me a kiss on the cheek with both of her hands gripping my forearms. She leans back, still holding on to me as she adds, "I'd say you don't want to be left alone with Mom." Her diagnosis sinks that knife a little deeper. "And I don't blame you."

"Go analyze someone else's psyche," I say, batting her hands away, once again opening my laptop and taking a seat on one of only two barstools lined up at the end of her counter.

"Just ... one hour," Cadence says and I wave her off, not bothering to look up and give her more reassurance. It's her house, her life. She's right, I don't want to be alone with my mother who looks like a shell of herself and is constantly crying or staring off at nothing. But I deserve just that.

The clicking of her heels is steady and determined, followed by the front door opening and closing. I can even hear her car turn on and then drive off. All the while I stare over my left shoulder, past the small living room with only a single sofa and one reading chair tucked into the corner. I have a direct line of sight out the glass doors to the patio and seated there, with the same mug she's had for hours, is my mother. The wicker furniture is comfortable enough, but I know the thin blanket my sister gave her can't be giving her much comfort since it lays on her lap and doesn't even cover her upper half.

Her nightgown is thin and she's got to be freezing, but the last three times we asked her to come in, she only shook her head and began crying again.

"I loved him. I loved him so much," she whispered the last time I went out there.

I wanted to talk to her, to try and process everything that's happened between the two of us, but she merely stared ahead blindly with a sad smile on her face, telling me she was counting all of her mistakes. She said she'll be out there for a while and not to mind her. With a small pat on my hand she looked me in the eye and added a *please* and another apology.

I debate on the likelihood that she'll come in if I go out there and ask her to again. It's slim to none, but I have to check on her.

Cadence still doesn't know it all. A single whispered conversation confirmed that our mother killed our father. My sister left, locked herself in the bathroom and then asked me for time. That was last night and this morning she's avoided any real conversation. We need to all sit down. The three of us know a secret no one else can ever know.

First, I need my mom to tell me what she's willing to let my sister know. It's obvious Cadence blames herself for something that she said triggered our mother. At least that's what she believes.

Whatever happens and whatever's spoken between us, I

want the three of us to know we still have each other. Given the current state of each of us individually ... I don't know how to make that happen.

All I know is that the police suspect someone else and have evidence that leads to that person.

You need to believe someone else did it. It's so much easier when someone else did it.

The consequences of delivering what feels like justice come with some sense of relief. A drunken attorney once told me that. I didn't think much of him back then, but oh how I wish those words were true right now and that I could, even for a split second, believe that someone other than my mother had done it. And that the police would find them, prosecute, and all would be right in the world. Save one more gravestone that shouldn't exist.

The morbid thought is interrupted by the buzzing of my phone, vibrating against the granite countertop. If it was anyone else, I'd just watch it ring and not answer.

But it's Cody. And after last night, the lone hour I gave him before coming back here to my sister's, I can't ignore him.

There's so much I need to tell him still. So much I want him to tell me.

"Cody?" I answer, holding my phone to my ear. I don't remember the last time I didn't answer on speaker. But with my mother in view, I don't want to risk her hearing any of this.

"How are you holding up?" His tone is caressing, and a

bit of it soothes me, a bit reminds me that so much is hurting.

"Not the best, not the worst," I tell him and stand up from the stool, leaning against the counter and stretching my back a bit. "Slept like shit and feel even shittier now."

My voice is deadpan but when Cody huffs a gruff laugh, the semblance of a smile tilts up my lips for a moment.

"Did you talk to the DA?"

"Yeah, she said I need to come in for counseling when I get back." I'm not given a chance to wonder how or why Cody would know that as I straighten. He doesn't give me the chance to wonder.

"There are some concerning thoughts from the PD back home too."

"Thoughts? Do they have a lead?" My pulse races and it hurts, physically, to feel it pounding in my chest.

"Can we talk about it in person?" Cody asks and I glance over my shoulder to watch my mother, thinking only of her being here and how that could be problematic with Cody coming over, but she's gone.

"Hold on," I say without thinking into the phone, pushing back the stool. The sound of the legs scraping is so loud Cody can probably hear it on the other end.

"You all right?" he asks but I'm too focused on the wicker chair and the puddle of blanket that blows slightly in the wind.

Where did she go? With my brow pinched I open the sliding glass door and call out, the phone pressed to my shoulder so Cody can't hear. "Mom?" I look around, searching to the left and to the right, but she's nowhere in sight.

"You okay?" Cody asks, calling out my name on the other end.

"I don't know," I tell him as I pick up my pace to go inside and call up the stairs for my mother.

It's quiet. Too quiet and my damned heart starts racing again.

"What's going on?" Cody asks at the same time I feel someone or something behind me.

When I turn, I fully expect it to be Marcus.

I don't have enough time to tell Cody who it is as the scream is ripped out of my throat and a bag thrown over my head.

With the dizziness, the clatter of my phone hitting the floor and the wind knocked out of me, I swear I try, but then there's another bash to my head.

Chapter 19

Marcus

There's always a calm before the storm. Some may think there's hope that it's over when the gray skies clear and the harsh wind silences its angry cries. I'm more than aware that hope is nowhere in sight and that the quiet moment is for readying, for preparing for the violence that's sure to come.

There's a reason I paired them together years ago. They were the only two people outside of the chaos who needed to stay there, in the blur on the edge.

She's only a little mouse, not even a pawn in the games. And yet … he couldn't hold on to her; he couldn't contain her. He couldn't keep her safe in his small, insignificant world.

My brother failed me. It's a betrayal of the worst kind. He's too careless, blinded by her and that's only going to cause more problems. I was too late, but he was supposed to be there with her. Cody was supposed to be watching her.

Without him, my pieces are limited and for the first time in years, I'm lacking. I'm behind. And it's all his fault.

"Tell me the moment you find her." My command is short, my tone even and just as placid as the autumn skies above me. The shades of red and orange bleed in my mind. Just as they did, one by one, massacred in the alley behind the abandoned warehouse, giving me every detail as I flayed the flesh from them. I had enough of them, watching the condo from their positions in windowless vans. So fucking obvious.

I slowly tortured one while the others watched.

Ask a simple question: *What car did they leave in?*

Get a simple answer: *A black Mercedes SUV.*

And ended his suffering with a gunshot to the back of his head.

Cody should be grateful for the use of the gun. It would have been better for me, for my sanity rather, to be a bit more harsh. But evidence will be on his side.

"Of course. Is there anything else?" The man I've hired who's on the other end of the line is a specialist of sorts. He acquires things ... certain precious things.

I swallow thickly, breathing in deep to stay levelheaded. *Is there anything else other than her?*

Time changes so much. There's always been more, far more important things than the little mouse who set me on this course. But now?

How could there possibly be anything other than her?

A stirring in my gut travels up my throat at the thought of her no longer existing. At the vision of her laying in a pool of her own blood like I've seen so many times with people in their last moments.

A strangled muffle echoes from the small closet. A quick glance proves the blood has leaked through the gauze once again. The bastard bit off his tongue and tried to swallow it.

An honest effort at suicide if ever I saw one.

I couldn't kill all of them. After all, someone had to talk. And he will, with two hands that work just fine.

"Did you have something to say now?" I ask him, not bothering to hide my face. He will die the slowest and most painful death I can conjure for the last words he spoke to me:

You're no ghost. You're no grim reaper.

You're just a man about to have his heart ripped out.

Any of the myriad enemies I have could be behind this. But there's only one I can tie each of these pricks to. Only one who would go after her entire family.

There's a reason she's supposed to be mine.

Everyone will pay.

This world will burn if they hurt her.

Chapter 20

Cody

"Tell me again what happened," Skov asks me. Again. The fucker doesn't know when to give up.

"They were already dead," I tell him. My tone is menacing and I pray to God for more control than I currently have while staring at the half-wit across the steel table from me. Every so often his left eye twitches. The dumb fuck can't control himself or his nerves.

"You're wasting time looking in the wrong direction and meanwhile, she's gone!"

"This isn't the first time she's been hiding out—"

Rage is unbecoming. Marcus told me that once. He cautioned me to contain it, but the worst bits of it boil over as I listen to this incapable fool imply that Delilah, my Delilah, left of her own free will.

"She was taken." The back of my teeth grind all while the words spill out. "Someone went to her sister's home, and took her."

"And the men there when we arrived? Did someone else kill them too?

"You just happened to be at the scene, your girlfriend missing, men dead on site ..." The dumb fuck who has it all wrong leans forward on the steel table, inching his face closer to mine.

The skin around my knuckles is tight as I clench my fist with the unbearable need to slam it into his smirk as he adds, "And you just happened to arrive after everything went down."

"There would be evidence," I grit out, although my vision blurs and I swear I see red. "Gunshot residue on my hands, perhaps, if I'd fired a fucking gun!" The words claw up my throat, each one raising the intensity as I stare him down. I stand up straight, throwing the metal chair back and listening to it clang as I scream at him. "Do your fucking job!"

The snide look on his face vanishes, fear flashing in his gaze as he backs away slowly. My shoulders hunch, my breathing coming and going as if I've just chased down the man responsible for all of this. Everything is tight and suffocating.

"I think it's best you calm down, Special Agent Walsh."

The statement isn't uttered with contempt, not with anything other than innate concern as he takes another step back.

Everything is so hot; I'm nothing but a caged animal in here. "I need to help find her." I barely get out the words before inhaling deep and slow. My head spins. "This can't be happening."

Where the fuck was he? Marcus killed them, but what about the woman he claims to love so much. Where the hell was he when she needed him?

With both hands behind my head, I turn my back to the interrogator. "I don't have time for this. I didn't do it and she's out there." The statement is simple and accurate.

"You just happened to get there ... and Miss Jones? She was already gone?" He repeats the same question but without the doubt and thinly veiled sarcasm. As if he's only double-checking facts.

Lowering my arms and picking up the chair, I tell him, "We were on the phone." The metal legs scratch against the floor as I put the chair back into place and take a seat. "She screamed, the phone dropped and I heard her screaming and then it was muffled and then ..."

Fuck, my hands tremble and I can't even look him in the eyes.

"A man's voice said something and then the line went out. I was close, but not close enough. The first thing I did was call in the disturbance."

Lie. The first thing I did was message Marcus. They have my phone. They'll have the number. *Fuck. Fuck. Fuck!*

He got there first and left a fucking mess for me to walk in on with cops trailing behind me.

"And when you got there, the suspects were exactly as they were when we found them?"

I can only nod. Nothing else is able to come out.

"It's one hell of a coincidence ..." Skov states, taking the seat across from me, leaning back casually.

"I'm aware," I say.

"You know we have to go through it all. Everything that was on you, your office, your records."

The filing cabinet flashes in front of my eyes. I nod then tell him, "I understand, but put men out there. Don't waste time." I plead with him instead of giving any thought to what's inside that filing cabinet in my office.

Please, for the love of God, don't look in the cabinet. It's locked. There's no reason to. Not unless they wanted to pin this on me. Not unless they tie the phone number I messaged to any other crimes.

Fuck, fuck. Doubt surrounds me and it's then that the interrogation door opens.

The other officer who took me in, I forget his name, strides in with heavy footsteps. His thin lips are pressed in a tight line and he flashes me a narrowed, untrusting gaze.

"I'm only going to ask you this once, and I expect full disclosure and honesty." The severity in his tone sends a prick of warning down my spine. "You only have one chance to keep your job, Special Agent Walsh. If there's even a possibility of that. How is the wanted criminal who goes by Marcus involved in all this? I want to know everything you know about him."

The first book belonged to Delilah. The second to Marcus.
The third is Cody's ... in a way. You'll have to read it and see.
This Love Hurts.
But I Need You.

And I Love You the Most,
Book Three,
the epic conclusion
in this darkly provocative, woven tale.

About the Author

Thank you so much for reading my romances. I'm just a stay at home Mom and an avid reader turned Author and I couldn't be happier.

I hope you love my books as much as I do!

More by Willow Winters
www.willowwinterswrites.com/books

Printed in Great Britain
by Amazon